About the Author

Logan Leigh Melrose is a British author who graduated in Film Studies at Staffordshire University. As a gay, trans male, Melrose specifies in writing queer love in numerous genres, touching on the vastness the LGBTQ+ community has to offer. When he's not writing, Melrose enjoys illustrating, reading, cuddling with his dogs and watching Netflix.

INFERNO HEARTS

Logan Leigh Melrose

Inferno Hearts

Vanguard Press

VANGUARD PAPERBACK

© Copyright 2023
Logan Leigh Melrose

A CIP catalogue record for this title is
available from the British Library.

ISBN 978-1-80016-808-4

Vanguard Press is an imprint of
Pegasus Elliot Mackenzie Publishers Ltd.
www.pegasuspublishers.com

First Published in 2022

Vanguard Press
Sheraton House Castle Park
Cambridge England

Printed & Bound in Great Britain

Acknowledgements

First and foremost, I would like to thank everyone who has supported this book. This is a project that has been in the works since 2020 and I went through a lot of highs and lows with it. I'm more than sure this book wouldn't have seen the light of day if it weren't for everyone who has encouraged me to never give up, in one way or another, from my mum who has always believed in me, encouraging me to never give up on my dreams, to all my friends, the absolute treasures that they are for reading through the painful early drafts and helping to keep me motivated. I would also like to thank my university tutor, John, for introducing me to my love of writing and storytelling. Lastly, I would like to thank you, the reader, for picking up this strange and wonderful book and giving it a chance! You are all amazing.

For the dreamers.

1
Dolor

Did you know angels and demons are real?

Well, we are.

You may think our destiny is decided upon a higher power but it's not. Yes, we have our God and our Devil, but where we end up is not up to them. Where we end up is completely decided upon our own hearts and the beliefs of the world.

The only rule in the afterlife is: you don't do enough good, you turn to a demon, and if you don't cause enough chaos, you turn to an angel.

Trust me, it's harder than it sounds.

So, our masters tell us what to do, give us missions, if you will.

My mission was simple.

Ruin Miles Green's life.

Break his heart. Isolate him. Make him hit rock bottom.

Believe it or not, it was always like this.

And it got very boring, very fast, if I might add.

For 150 years it was my job to be the heartbreaker.

My job was by far the hardest.

It's easy enough for Pollution to make mankind destroy their own world, for Greed to make a man selfish, and Wrath make a woman cold-hearted.

People are naturally drawn to the darkness; it's a lot easier to sit in the dark than walk into the light.

But for me, I had to bring people up to that light, make them feel the best they have in years, just to toss them back further into the darkness than they ever had been before.

I had broken the hearts of thousands, had hundreds cry over me, and had many sink into despair wondering why I cursed such misery upon them.

I was never to be an angel.

This all started long ago when I was still alive, long before my immortal life as a demon began.

I came from a broken home, a bastard—an old term now, I know, but I was born in 1836, so shut it. I lived with my mother in a shabby old cottage until I was eleven. She clearly loved me deeply, working three jobs to keep that leaky roof over my head. I, however, was cold to the feeling. I ran away to find my father—her heart: broken.

I was ridiculously better off with him. After eleven years of my mother telling me my father was a crazy drunk, it turned out he was, in fact, a Lord. Still a drunk, yes—but a Lord! Lord Henry Valentine of Linlithgow.

At seventeen, I loved one of our maids for three weeks then accused her of witchcraft. Why? For the simple fact that she bored me. I watched her burn. Her heart: broken and stopped beating completely.

At twenty-two, I cheated on my then-fiancée with my dying father's wife. Two hearts broken, two that soon stopped beating. One from suicide, the other from heart failure—you figure out which is which.

Twenty-six, I drove my father's widow out of the manor. Homeless and heartbroken.

And finally, to the bittersweet end, at thirty-four, my then-wife stabbed me seventeen times in the heart after she caught me having an affair with our best maid.

I was a Lord. I was wealthy and handsome.

But nothing compared to what I had when I died.

They called me Dolor—Demon of Heartache and Pain.

2
Dolor

Did you know Cupid used to be a demon? He used to have my job. Until one day he simply had enough, said he felt bad for hurting all those people. So, off he went, without punishment—went off to become a precious angel.

I wouldn't give up that easily.

Being so cruel was an art.

My last mission was quite the disappointment, however. It required a lot of something called T-E-X-T-I-N-G. I never even saw the girl I broke up with.

It did make me frightfully worried that all modern-day relationships would take place over these screens. But luckily, to my relief, my next mission did involve physical interaction.

So, there was the next victim on my list: Miles Green.

Back in the day, this mission would've been a piece of cake, just love him then accuse him of being homosexual. You'd break his heart in a flash.

But the human race had changed since I last stepped foot on it—this strange message box being one of them—being gay was no longer frowned upon. I had to work harder.

And how much fun that ended up being.

Miles was twenty-two at the time—living in Cambridge away from his parents as he studied English Literature at the university there.

That was my way in.

October 19th, a new academic year, and Miles' last year at the university. I had a year to get this done.

Duck soup.

I went to the university; its long lawns and ancient architecture were clearly compensating for the old phoneys in the place who claimed to be teachers.

Professor Addington was in charge of English Literature, teacher of Class 17 in the English Department—Miles' class.

He wouldn't be teaching for much longer.

It was seven thirty; no students around yet.

But our chubby professor was already in, working in his office.

I got a few odd stares from other teachers as I headed to the old brute's room.

Could it have been what I was wearing?

I suppose people don't often go to the University of Cambridge wearing a black leather jacket, skinny jeans, and perhaps a little too much eyeliner.

The old farts were all too scared of me to say anything about it—to my face anyway.

I knocked on the door and he called for me to come in.

"Who are you?" he asked.

I simply told him I was his replacement.

He looked confused for a moment.

Then scared—he saw something in my eyes that no man should see.

Hell.

With just a click of my fingers, the old man lit up like a bonfire, entirely consumed by flames.

Within seconds the fires burned out and old Professor Addington was nothing but ash.

Goodbye, sir.

After a bit of clearing up—dusting the ash into the bin and making the office my own—I was all set.

With another click, I changed myself into something more professor-like: simple shirt, blazer and trousers would do. The first shirt button had to be undone though, it always had to be, too tight otherwise.

I was now the new Head of the English Department—and no one would question where old Addington went because, in their minds, he simply retired.

Nine o'clock. I made my way into the English Literature lecture room.

All the students were already seated.

"Good morning class!" I exclaimed. Everyone remained silent.

I stood at the front of the class and took the chalk in my hand.

May as well use the name I had as a human.

I started to write on the chalkboard.

"I am Professor David Valentine. I will be your new Literature teacher."

No one replied.

Did you know Shakespeare is a demon?

Pride.

I picked up the paper register on the desk and began to call out people's names.

"Abigail," I called. She simply replied: "Here."

Today's youth are a lazy lot.

I continued to go down the list: there was Emma and Liam, Will and Zoe, Jack and Chloe, Lily and James.

When did names become so dull?

What happened to names like Asteria, Fraser, Tigris, Claudius?

Names that screamed individuality.

Now it seemed like children's names were chosen at random out of a hat by someone with no imagination.

I continued down the list and there, finally, was his name.

"Miles," said I. I looked up to see what he looked like.

No one answered to the name.

"Miles?" I repeated.

Miles, Latin for soldier.

The Mighty Medieval Knight.

At least one student here had a semi-decent name.

"He's probably in the library," said one of the students—Sarah, I think.

"Well, what's he doing in there?" I asked, a bit more frustration in my voice than needed.

"He's always in there," said another student.

"Thinks the class is too easy for him," said another.

"And Professor Addington did nothing about it?"

No one answered.

I huffed. It was going to be a long day.

I told the students to get on with whatever studying they needed to do while I went to sort out this Miles situation.

No hearts would be broken if he was always hiding out in the library.

After getting directions from a passing teacher, I made my way to the library, which did include me going out into the pouring rain.

The mission already seemed to be going from bad to worse, the last thing I needed was my hair to be as flat as a pancake and my eyeliner dripping down my face.

I made it inside the library, shaking my soaked hair like a dog and wiping as much as the eyeliner off my face as I could; it somehow just made it worse. The librarian—I assumed—stared at me with wide eyes.

Cow.

I gave her a smug grin before I stormed into the forest of books.

It took some searching, I glanced down each aisle of bookshelves as I stormed my way through.

I finally found my way to the back of the library, and by my amazement Miles was sitting there—reading.

"Miles Green?"

He looked up at me.

He was rather scrawny, not like the other boys in the class who were clearly compensating for something.

"Aren't you supposed to be in my class right now?" I asked rhetorically but he answered anyway.

"I work better alone."

"I never said you had to work with anyone, just that you had to be in the classroom."

Miles looked confused about something. "Professor Addington used to make us do team projects together."

I huffed in amusement.

"Well, I'm not old Professor Addington. You can work alone."

He still seemed hesitant. Why did I have to be stuck with a coward?

"The others don't like me," he whispered.

I sighed.

"You can stay here—just for today, though. I want you back in class tomorrow."

He nodded; he was trying not to smile but he was so relieved it was hard for him not to show it—or maybe it was the smudged eyeliner he was trying not to laugh at.

"Thank you, sir."

I gave a quick nod before I headed back into the maze.

Step One of being successful as the Demon of Heartache and Pain: Compromise for the victim.

You must straight away show you're on their side, to gain trust.

3
Miles

It was still dark out when I left the flat. Despite it being flat 27, I lived on the top floor. The numbers in this student accommodation establishment refused to go in order. Flat 505 was on the ground floor. Believe me, I'm not exaggerating when I say it took me five hours to find my room on my first day.

There was an icy mist over every surface; it felt like fire when my hand pushed open the iron gate to the building. I always forgot to take gloves with me, although they always ended up redundant anyway. My parents would've blabbered on at me for not taking such a necessity on a cold morning such as this, but I found many things my parents once told me while growing up also became redundant once I was living alone at university—cleaning the home every other day, eating a big breakfast each morning, managing your money— all things that worked for some, but not others, not me. My flat was small enough to keep clean and tidy standards once a week. Coffee was enough to keep me going until lunch, and I scraped by with enough student loan to keep me going while I saved over half of it to hopefully one day move away to New York.

The disposable cup heated my pasty hands. The steam of hot coffee wafted up inside my nostrils as I walked briskly through the fog, each step was met with a crunching of minuscule ice crystals that had formed on the pavement overnight. The few others who walked past me in the opposite direction were much slower paced, waddling like penguins. They worried about the risk of slipping, but I had no time to slow down to prevent such a risk. I had places to go and people to not see.

The university looked more like a graveyard when I arrived: the fog swarmed most of the building to appear more like a tomb than a learning facility. I walked along the side path, sheltered under the archway which gave the illusion of it being warmer. A professor passed me; I didn't know her, but I ducked my head regardless to avoid any unnecessary greeting or eye contact. Every term for the past three years I was up and down this path in the early hours of the morning. I remember the first few months of doing so, every professor, cleaner and receptionist questioned why I arrived over an hour early each morning. Every time I made the excuse that it was the only bus I could catch that got here, none of them questioned me further; what else is there to say? But I never took the bus here, or cycled, or drove. I didn't need to get here early, I wanted to. I wanted to get in before the rush of students did. All of their rustling and barging. I'd much rather have to wake up at half five every morning than deal with that.

I continued past the university until I reached the library. Its tall stature dominated the city skyline but it wasn't intimidating walking up those steps and through the swinging door, more like coming home. It was toasty inside, the thick brick walls kept in all the heat from the previous day. The mix of ancient, insulated walls and modern central heating made this the cosiest place to be in the cold seasons, but then again was also hellish to be in when it was summer. I snuck my way past the receptionist by the library entrance as she dealt with the crumbs her bagel spilt down her cardigan. The library wasn't open till nine a.m., but she's never caught me. The librarian did though: Nell. She caught me in there during the first week. She never did mind though, knowing I was genuinely in there to read and study, not just as using it as a hideaway to skip classes, although it was that too.

She cleared her throat, getting my attention. She gestured to the cup in my hand.

"Ah, yes." I nodded. I tipped the last few droplets of coffee into my mouth; by now it had gone lukewarm and lost its flavour. I tossed the empty cup into the bin. It was Nell's one rule: no eating or drinking while in the library. Some of the books in here were very rare, beyond valuable. You would be paying for the damages with your soul.

"Good to see you back." Nell smiled. She had aged. Last summer she looked like a middle-aged mother, tired but kept fit with house chores and perhaps yoga or jogging. Now dark bags hung under her eyes, and the large spectacles didn't help, magnifying the effects of stress and time.

"You too." I sighed. I hadn't got up this early in months; getting back into the routine tired me.

Our brief exchange ended as I tiptoed my way through the forest of books. Titles and authors breezed past, all of them catching my eye and drawing me in. Nell had quite a few new books in, and lucky for me, I had the whole year to get through them. Soon enough, I was back in my happy place. Back of the library, sitting at one of the empty tables. I nestled down, wrestling with my backpack as I took it off and put it down by my feet, keeping it close. Even here, I still dread the thought of someone running off with my things. I took out my notebook and the novel I borrowed from the last academic year. Nell always trusted me to bring them back. I flicked delicately through the pages until I met my bookmark and I continued on my adventure.

I was wrapped up in a whole other world, one of magic and mystery. With characters such as these that lie within the pages, what do I have to interact with the real world for? I was getting towards the end but I didn't want to leave, say goodbye to this new world I found myself comfortable in, with these characters I now recognised more as friends than fictional. What was to happen in these last few pages, these last few paragraphs, would change me forever.

"Miles Green?" said an unfamiliar voice.

I looked up to see who the voice belonged to and saw a tall, slender man. He was too old to be a student, but too attractive to be a professor. Everyone who taught here had more folds of wrinkles than a sphynx cat. His pale skin contrasted his pitch-black blazer and trousers. The exposed skin of his chest that his shirt revealed was something the headmaster here wouldn't prohibit at all.

"Aren't you supposed to be in my class right now?"

Professor David Valentine. Why did I forget who it was? Suddenly I didn't find him attractive any more. Nope. Not at all.

I shook my head. "I work better alone."

He didn't seem impressed with my response at all, the whites of his eyes exposed as they rolled.

"I never said you had to work with anyone, just that you had to be in the classroom."

I was stuck on what to say, I tried to think of when Valentine ever taught our class, but I hadn't been there in so long that it wasn't surprising that old Professor Addington had been replaced. He laughed when I mentioned him and went on trying to convince me to join the class. It made me feel sick to my stomach thinking about being surrounded by all the boisterous students in that lecture room.

Something changed in Valentine; his voice softened. "You can stay here. Just for today though. I want you in class tomorrow."

The silky tone instantly soothed me, and I nodded, relieved to have the rest of the day to myself, able to compose myself for the hell of tomorrow.

"Thank you, sir."

A smile started to curve the corners of my lips.

He simply nodded at me and walked away, disappearing behind a bookshelf.

4
Dolor

The rest of that day was long and tedious, and I wanted to die! Again.

There was no sight of Miles the whole time. I asked Professor Oxley (Head of the University) about the boy during my lunch break, and he simply said they let the boy do as he pleased. That he gets the work done, and done well, and that no one saw an issue with him being alone. This was going to be more difficult than I had hoped, but I needed a challenge; the missions were getting too easy. Maybe that's why it was assigned to me.

At the end of the university day, I made my way to my new human home. Yes, it was Professor Addington's manor.

I wasn't going to let such a big and spacious house go to waste. It wasn't like he was going to be needing it any more.

The old brute lived alone, so it was easy enough for me to take the place as my own.

I clicked my fingers and the front gate opened. The driveway was gravelled and circular with a water fountain in the centre.

These teachers get paid way too much considering the lack of teaching they actually do.

I walked up to the house: cream-white bricks with two pillars supporting the archway.

Now, this was the place for me.

The front door was at least seven feet high; I looked puny in comparison.

I felt ever so at home.

The manor was sparkling clean and modern, but with Victorian hints through the wooden spiral staircase banister, the dark patterned furniture, and a whole room dedicated to books upon books.

I felt like the luckiest demon in all of Hell.

I still had Miles to deal with however, otherwise I wouldn't be a demon at all.

That was tomorrow's problem though.

A demon has to relax.

The kitchen was filled with all sorts of fancy equipment: a De'Longhi coffee machine, a Zeppoli kettle, and Zenshi teapot for loose tea leaves.

It didn't take long for me to help myself.

In one of the cupboards, there was a selection of different teas and coffees: Liberica coffee, Robusta coffee, Arabica coffee, Bourbon espresso coffee,

Breakfast Blend coffee, Earl Grey, English Rose loose tea, Piccadilly Blend, jasmine, peppermint, golden camomile, spiced chai, dark chocolate, white chocolate, mango, apple.

The list goes on and on and I don't want to bore you with me whoring over hot beverages.

The cupboard was completely filled (neatly) with types of coffee beans, tea bags, and leaves.

There were so many choices.

So many possibilities.

I decided to go with the golden camomile, about the only thing that gave me a warm feeling in the heart.

After the tea leaves had brewed in the steaming water, I poured the tea into a mug and took myself some dark chocolate biscuits before I headed upstairs into the master bedroom. I saw it had a fireplace, an armchair and small coffee table.

I settled the cup on the table, biscuits in my mouth as I sat down.

I tapped my foot on the floor and the fireplace lit with a hot flame.

I simply sat there for the rest of the evening, munching on biscuits, and sipping at the tea that made me feel all fuzzy and warm inside.

Even though I was a demon, some human things are quite enjoyable.

5
Miles

After so long at home, not doing much more than reading and napping, being back at university was a headache. Adjusting back to an old familiar routine, the sights and smells instantly sending your brain into overdrive that today was going to be hard. It was, even though I spent most of the day in the library. I ventured out once, just for lunch. There were far too many students in the cafeteria for me to even think about going in there, so I ate out with the only friend I had. Billy.

He was a few years older than me and had always been like a big brother to me, my guardian angel in dark times. He never failed to meet me on time outside the university gates; from there, we went to a little café down the road. It was quiet, cosy, independent. Not like one of these busy chain cafés. I hadn't seen Billy in quite a while, at least a couple of months, but then I did confine myself to my apartment. While other students went home to their families for the summer break, I remained. It was a comfort to be around a friend again, or more like a family member at this point. He sure was more like my family than my real blood relatives.

We ate and we drank before leaving the café, strolling back to the university. I walked as slowly as I could; I didn't want to go back. I wanted to talk with Billy all day. But even then, he was one to encourage me to do things that scared me. He ushered me back inside, almost in a mocking tone, just as I imagine a brother would.

The headache was brewing on my walk home, my brain on strike from the sudden venture out into the real world. I walked briskly back to the student accommodation and straight into my apartment, locking the door. I needed my bed, I needed sleep. I walked right through, pulling off my bag and jacket, tossing them aside as I walked into my bedroom. I kicked off my shoes, shortly after collapsing onto the bed, faceplanting the pillow.

When I awoke, it was pitch-black outside. I was disorientated by tiredness and the loss of time. With a groan, I sat up and grabbed my phone from the bedside table. It was 8.46 p.m. I had slept for over four hours. I would've gone back to sleep, but my stomach growled with hunger. So, I got up. The room spun for a second, I balanced myself before I walked towards the cramped kitchen. There wasn't much in the fridge but luckily, I still had a spare pasty. I unwrapped it before tossing it into the microwave. I spent my time waiting for the microwave to ping by flicking through the TV channels until I found something half decent on. Good timing, pasty was done. I went to grab it out with my bare hand, instantly I drew back with a wince as it burnt the tips of my fingers. I took out a small plate from the cupboard, holding it in front of the microwave as I quickly tossed the pasty onto it, quickly enough for it to not burn too much. I took my first bite as I made my way over to the sofa, plunking myself down, getting cosy into the cushions. My eyes were fixed on the TV screen as I indulged in my late-night dinner and before I knew it, it was almost midnight. I spent too much time watching TV, and now the consequence was to feel like shit in the morning.

This year was going to be more difficult than I thought.

6
Dolor

The next morning I arose at approximately 9.35 a.m.; I was late for class.

But no worry.

As I clicked my fingers, the clock on the bedside table turned back by two hours, as did the clocks everywhere else. Now if anything, I would be early.

I let out a morning yawn and got myself in my robe before I headed downstairs. In the kitchen, I made myself a simple black coffee. I needed all the caffeine I could get if I was to deal with all the Miles bullshit that day.

I stood outside on the porch as the sun emerged over the houses.

As I looked out on this new world, I began to dwell on what would become of me if I didn't succeed.

The demon life was all I knew.

I couldn't let all that be taken away from me because of one stubborn boy.

But no matter because that wouldn't be the case.

A challenge, yes.

But not impossible.

As the first lesson began, I was disappointed yet not surprised to see Miles wasn't present.

That boy had some nerve to test me.

I know he was twenty-two and technically an adult, but I was 184 years old, so I think it was okay to call him boy.

I took the register and got the class busy with their novella pitches while I went to deal with the exceedingly irritating problem I had.

Step Two of being successful as the Demon of Heartache and Pain: Sympathise with the victim.

Back I went down the long aisle of books and old dusty oak.

Once again there he was, sitting at one of the back tables. The desk lamp pointed towards whatever garbage he was reading.

I approached and stood there silently for a moment, hands behind my back.

But he just continued reading, he didn't even glance up.

I cleared my throat and finally, he acknowledged my presence.

"Oh. Hi, sir."

Hi sir, my arse.

"Didn't I tell you to be in class today?"

"I'm sorry—I was going to. I just..." Miles trailed off.

"You feel like you don't belong in that class?" I tried my best to find the root of his insecurities. My only way to be able to truly sympathise with him was to know what was really wrong.

"Not so much the class itself as the—"

"People in it?" I interrupted.

Miles looked speechless for a moment.

"Yeah." He finally exhaled.

I let out a sigh, giving the indication I felt sorry for the boy.

"Look, I know it's hard being stuck in a room with people you don't like. How do you think I feel in the staffroom?"

I saw Miles trying to hold back a chuckle, but he still couldn't stop himself from smiling.

"Come to class; you don't have to work or sit near anyone, and I promise I won't let anyone speak wrongly to you."

Miles was silent. I could see him thinking it through.

"Won't that just make things worse?" Miles spoke out. "I mean, won't they just see me as the teacher's pet?"

"Is there something wrong with that?" I smirked.

Miles admitted there was nothing wrong with actually being the teacher's pet and finally agreed to come back to class, knowing I would keep my promise.

Dealing with things back in the class was actually easy on my part.

This teaching thing was simple, I don't know why people had to go through so much work to become a professor. I knew all there was to know about the literature they were learning about, mainly because I was present in all the eras the authors had been.

I was also able to keep my promise to Miles.

Throughout it was obvious Miles was uncomfortable, timid.

He was on edge for most of the lecture, worried that at any moment he would be mocked or threatened.

And there were moments a student or two was going to bully the boy, but at those times I simply got the attention of the whole class, distracting the bullies from their mission without having to embarrass Miles.

I could see Miles appreciated that as well, some spark in his eyes, the corner of his lips turning up.

He was clearly beginning to trust me.

The food at this place was vile.

Back when I was a boy, the teachers were given the good stuff while we ate gruel.

Everyone here ate gruel.

One of the lumpy, greasy dinner ladies slopped on the food that resembled her onto my tray, and then I proceeded to find myself somewhere to sit.

I refused to sit near Professor Finky with her constant bickering.

Or Professor McLaughlin with her weird obsessions with short, bearded men.

And especially not Professor Lord with his spitting problem when he talked.

I continued to walk down the aisle of tables.

It was then I noticed Miles sitting all alone at a table of four in the corner.

And surrounding him was a couple of the students from the class. They were giving him trouble.

I could hear them calling him names, saying how cowardly he was for skipping class.

Miles looked ever so scared; he kept his head down and just let them walk all over him.

Step Three of being successful as the Demon of Heartache and Pain: Protect the victim.

I walked up to the table Miles was at.

I barged my way in between the table and the students, instantly stopping them in their tracks.

"I think it would be best you stop bothering the boy and get yourselves something to eat, don't you agree?" I warned.

The students simply walked away; I'd let them off easy this time.

I turned to face Miles who was looking up at me with almost complete amazement.

"Mind if I sit?" I asked.

Miles shook his head and invited me to join him. I sat opposite.

For moments there was a still silence between us before Miles broke it.

"Why are you helping me?"

"Well I'm your teacher, isn't that my job?" I said as I pushed away my tray in disgust.

I'd rather starve.

"To teach me, yes. Not to help me with personal matters. No other teacher does."

"Well, I'm not like the other teachers."

I nudged the tray further away; I could still smell the foul thing.

"Would you prefer I didn't help?"

"No," Miles answered quickly, too quickly and he could tell.

Seems I'd finish this mission by the end of the week.

"Well, there you have it. You continue being the bright kid you are, and I'll make sure no one messes with you."

He couldn't resist and gave a cheerful smile. "You'd do that for me?"

"Well, yes." I rested my chin on my hand. "I know what it's like, being tormented, teased. It's not fair." I pouted like an upset toddler. "You deserve to have the best last year here, and I'll make sure you do."

Miles' smile continued to grow as he spoke. "Thanks, sir."

"Don't mention it."

It was five p.m., end of the university day.

I made my way to the teacher's car park where my precious baby was waiting.

My car, that is.

A black 1960 DB4 GT Zagato Aston Martin. A beautiful piece of machinery with a white stripe sandwiched between two red stripes over the bonnet and roof. As well as a white and red stripe on both sides at the bottom.

I got the beauty back in the late sixties while on a mission.

I've had her ever since.

I drove out of the car park but idled with the engine spluttering away outside the university building as Miles walked out.

He didn't notice me, or the car. Or anything, for that matter. He quickly walked down the university steps, hugging books close to his chest and made his way down the pavement, presumably in the direction of his home.

At this point, I believed this mission would be easy.

The boy was timid, yes.

And preferred to be left alone.

But mainly out of fear. I had to just continue showing him he could trust me, that I could be his rock.

I would be the only one he could fall back on in his miserable world.

I stayed till the boy was nothing but a speck in the distance.

At that point I pulled away from the side of the pavement, the engine roaring as I accelerated and made my own way home.

There was a storm that night.

Brash and lurid.

There was no better way to spend it than by the fireplace with some more of my favourite camomile tea and a decent-sized slice of salted caramel cheesecake.

Oh, it was a good afterlife.

It was a cosy feeling, being inside in the warmth while it was cold and pouring it down outside.

The blazing fire glowed against the dark walls of my bedroom.

After all the tea and cake was consumed, I raised from the armchair and made my way to clean the dishes downstairs, but before I turned to leave the room, I noticed a crimson glow outside the window.

It caught my attention; I stood in front of the tall window and looked out.

Below, behind the fencing that surrounded the manor were two familiar figures.

Their bodies were pitch-black and surrounded in a dark swirling mist.

And their eyes, piercing red, which were also swathed in a mist of crimson.

Nuntius and Perfidus were their names.

Satan's messenger and right-hand demon, respectively.

They usually check up on demons to make sure they follow through with their missions, but they never usually do so with me.

It was odd, but not troubling. I knew I would get the mission done.

They stared at me with their burning eyes, and I stared back.

It was short-lived, however, as their human-like silhouettes morphed and shrunk until Nuntius transformed into a crow, and Perfidus a Dobermann dog.

The last to change were their eyes.

Their sharp red eyes continued to stare into my soul until they went about their business as if they were a real crow and dog.

I was left with a shiver down my spine and a doubting question in the back of my mind.

Didn't they trust me?

7
Dolor

Wednesday. It was 8.47 a.m. as I was approaching the university.

The roads were clear, and my Aston was thriving.

As was I with one of my favourite cassettes blasting through the speakers.

I may have been speeding… But no matter!

The university building was in view. I planned to turn into the staff car park, but it was then I noticed the heads of students turn in my direction.

Perhaps I was driving too recklessly?

Maybe my music was too loud?

They stepped back and it was revealed to me they were surrounding Miles, who was now a mess on the ground with his books ripped up, scattered.

Even for a demon, it was a sad sight to see.

I jolted the steering wheel to the right and slammed my foot on the brakes, parking (not so well) at the side on the pavement by the group of students. The pure sound of 70s rock music still pulsing out the Aston's stereo.

Anyway, enough side-tracking...

Frankly, my amazing driving had already scared a few of the students off, but some remained.

I left the car running as I stepped out.

I pulled off my sunglasses and tucked one of the temples into my shirt.

I approached the remaining members of the group.

"Well, that's not a very nice way to treat a classmate, is it?"

They apologised quietly, more out of fear than being genuine.

"I do believe you're adults now, but you're sure as hell not acting like it. Now clear off!" I waved my hand at them, signalling for them to go inside, which they did.

Miles was looking a sight for fore eyes on the damp concrete, although he seemed too ashamed, embarrassed to look up.

I walked over and held my hand out.

After a little hesitation, he took it and I gently pulled him up off the ground.

"Are you okay?" I asked softly.

Miles simply nodded. He looked down at the mess of his books on the ground, his expression would make anyone's heartbreak.

"Don't worry about them," I reassured him. I leant down and gathered all the books and ripped out pages. "You get to class, and I'll have these sorted for you."

Miles looked puzzled.

"I don't think they're fixable, sir."

"Oh, just you wait and see." I smiled. "Go on, I'll be with you shortly."

Miles nodded once again before he headed inside.

Meanwhile, I got back in the Aston to park it safely in the staff car park.

I really was able to fix the books.

I am a demon after all; we're as good at fixing things as we are at breaking them.

One by one, I took each book in my lap, sorted all the pages in the right order before I clicked my fingers together.

And there you have it, the books all back intact.

I collected all the books and exited the car, locking it before heading for the back entrance of the building.

I had a bad feeling Miles wouldn't be in class.

He was going to be back in the library for sure.

But to my amazement, there he was when I entered the lecture room.

Back of the class, keeping to himself as everyone else chatted amongst themselves.

I wandered up the stairs, approaching him, not disturbing the others from their social talk.

I gently placed the now-fixed books upon his desk chair and his face lit up.

"All fixed."

"How did you…?" He was astonished.

"I have a few tricks up my sleeve."

I managed to make my way next to Miles in the queue at lunch. He seemed relieved to see me there with him, perhaps he didn't feel so alone.

He thanked me for fixing his books, and once again expressed his amazement at how I managed to do it.

It was then we were first in the queue and the usual slop was dumped onto our trays.

"Do they serve this crap every day?"

Miles laughed softly.

"You get used to it."

I cringed at the sight of the food.

"I'd rather not have to."

Miles' tray was filled before mine and he turned to find a table, but his face dropped.

I turned to see that the problem was the pupils from class.

They were minding their own business, but they were all gathered right in the middle of the aisle of tables, blocking the way.

Presumably Miles knew soon as he tried to walk past, they'd be beating him down to the floor again.

I leaned in to whisper to him.

"Walk past them."

Miles said he couldn't.

"Do you trust me?"

He hesitated.

"Walk past them and I promise you they won't bother you," I said with confidence.

Miles looked back at the crowd of pupils then back at me, and I repeated. "Do you trust me?"

"I do." Miles nodded. He picked up his tray from the side before he headed towards the crowd.

Now, of course, I knew the kids were going to bother him. They would hit his tray out of his hands and call him a freak.

It was nothing I couldn't prevent though.

As Miles headed into the crowd, I clicked my fingers, and the pupils were punished into a trance.

Nothing drastic that would cause other people to notice, it just stopped them from being able to see Miles.

And just as quickly as it started, Miles was in the clear and sat down.

I joined him soon after and he had the biggest smile of relief on his face.

"How did you know they'd leave me alone?"

I shrugged. "I just knew. And now you do too because you trusted me."

"And I always will."

And just like that, I was more than halfway to stealing Miles' heart.

Step Four of being successful as the Demon of Heartache and Pain: Gain the victim's trust.

8
Miles

This was precisely why I came to university in the early hours of the morning.

"Hey, queer," they called me. Devilish grins on their faces as they approached. They didn't hesitate to slap the books out of my hands. They fell to the ground so effortlessly because of how clammy my palms were. Why did I have to sleep through my alarm this morning?

"Why you always hiding?" Joe laughed. He was always the one to give me trouble. He would purposely waste his own time to bother me. He tripped me up, kicking the back of my ankle and I went down like a ton of bricks. Everything from then on was a blur. All I could feel, all I could see, was pain. Sudden bursts of agony in my spine and shins as they kicked me over and over and over again. Their laughs were like singeing acid, the tearing of book pages was like they were ripping out my own heart. There was nothing I could do. I just lay there, curled up with my hands covering my face as I sobbed so loudly that I couldn't breathe.

Their brutality slowed down. Their kicks softened before coming to a stop completely, I didn't understand why, maybe they were just toying with me. Either way, I stayed in a ball. That was until I heard music. Loud, familiar music. The screeching of tyres caused several people to run off. I looked up to see only Joe and his best friend stood there, and in front of them the nicest car I had ever seen. I didn't have time to think of who it belonged to as Professor Valentine swiftly stepped out and approached us.

"We'll, that's not a very nice way to treat a classmate, is it?" He tucked his sunglasses into his shirt. I kept my head up as best I could to see what was going on. Joe and his friend had never obeyed Professor Addington, but here now with Valentine, they were intimidated.

"S-sorry," they both muttered to the Professor.

"Not to me, him," he growled. They both turned down to me and repeated their apology louder.

"I do believe you're adults now, but you're sure as hell not acting like it. Now clear off!"

He glared at the two of them as they skulked away like dogs with their tails between their legs.

My eyes stayed on the professor the whole time, even though his harsh words weren't aimed at me, I couldn't help but be fearful. Yet, his eyes were soft when they met mine. He leant down and held out his hand to me with such grace that he seemed to be in slow motion. I took his hand and he smoothly brought me up onto my feet. He was making sure I was okay, but I didn't care about myself. The books, Nell's books. They lay like fallen soldiers on the battlefield. My attention was brought back to the professor as he came into view. He collected the torn books on the ground and stood before me.

"You get to class, and I'll have these sorted for you."

He might have been ravishing, but he was delusional.

"I don't think they're fixable, sir." I said as I looked at him, puzzled. He simply gave me a look with those dark, mysterious eyes of his, as if he had something cunning planned. He told me to go to class, and before I could say anything he was walking back to his car.

I wanted to go to the library. I was going to go straight there, screw going to class to get beaten up once more. But as I stood between the library and the English Department, I hesitated. I couldn't go back to Nell empty-handed; she was expecting those books to be returned, and although it was foolish to think the professor could fix them, the way he looked at me made me truly believe that he was capable of doing it somehow.

The class fell silent as I walked in; everyone looked at me. I cleared my throat before I walked on, going to the back of the room, and sitting at my small desk. I knew they were talking about me, about what happened outside with Joe and the professor. I could tell from their murmurs and glances back. It didn't last too long though. The professor was already back with my books. Everyone went back to their normal conversations as he walked straight towards me and gently placed the books before me. I had absolutely no words. They were beyond fixed, they looked brand new.

He joined me at lunch. I don't know why it comforted me so much. It was a similar comfort I felt being around Billy, expect with the professor there was a mystery to him that I couldn't quite solve. Once the food was put on my tray, I turned to get us a table, only to see Joe and the others once again: they blocked the way to an empty corner table.

"Walk past them."

I felt his hot breath against my ear. The sudden warmth startled me, and I quickly turned to him.

"What?" I looked to the crowd, then back to Valentine. "I can't."

No matter how badly I tried to convince him I couldn't do it, he refused to give in, and then once more, he gave me that look. His eyes a void into endless possibilities, hopes, dreams.

"Do you trust me?" His voice melted.

"I do."

9

Dolor

The following day was pretty bland, in all fairness.

The students who usually pick on Miles seemed to mind their own business that day, left him alone.

I continued to unleash my brilliance of knowledge of the literature world upon the living souls, and already I was seeing my steps to being successful at this job was coming into full effect.

Throughout the entire day's lesson, Miles was looking at me.

Not the 'I'm paying attention' look like from the other students.

Actually *looking* at me. Observing, admiring me.

This would be my quickest mission yet.

The boss would be pleased.

I took a break from Miles at lunch, however.

Two days in a row sitting with a student at lunch would look suspicious to anyone on the outside of this operation.

I decided to have my lunch in the staff room instead, where it was empty.

The rest of the professors still ate in the usual dining hall with the students.

I was all alone. The way I liked it.

I had stashed some camomile tea bags into my satchel.

Yes, I know it's a man-bag.

But when I got it in 1984, it was called a satchel so deal with it.

Besides, it was designer, genuine leather.

Only the best.

Anyway, I had enough of the slop they served at that university.

Having lunch in the staff room meant I could have whatever I wanted.

So, I took one of the scrumptious tea bags and plopped it into the mug while I waited for the kettle to boil.

I went on to make myself an ever so simple but tasteful ham and brie sandwich.

I had brought all the ingredients from home because I knew whatever was in the cupboards of the staff room would most likely be out of date and simply not to my higher taste.

After the art-making of the sandwich and the tea bag had fully brewed, I sat down at the table meant for eight.

I sighed with pure bliss at the sight and smells before me. This would be the best lunch I'd had at this dull university ever.

As I took my first sip at the tea, in burst the headmaster ruining my peace and quiet.

"Ah! Valentine!" the fat man bellowed with his hideous grey moustache curtained over his top lip. "All alone, I see."

I pretended to be amused by him.

"Correct."

He asked if he could join, I felt I had no choice but to accept.

He sat right opposite me. Just the sight of him put me off my food. This man looked more of a disgrace than Professor Addington did before he was nothing but ash.

I continued to sip at my tea silently.

I'll enjoy my sandwich once he's gone, I thought.

But the old man stayed for what seemed like an eternity, waffling on about funds for the university, new measures to take for students who acted out of line, his favourite types of meat. I have to say, I don't know how that last one came into conversation.

And it was then that his own piggy eyes caught sight of my sandwich.

With his greasy paws, he grabbed one of the slices and bloody ate it!

Oh, I could've killed him.

It felt like a bomb was ticking away inside me.

"Thank you," he chuckled, obviously assuming the sandwich was for anyone.

"Quite all right." I spoke through gritted teeth.

The balloon-shaped man flicked the crumbs off his shirt that was two sizes too small then arose. He wished me a good rest of the day then left.

Oh, that man had it coming to him. Sooner or later, I would have my revenge.

I looked down at the other half of the sandwich. I could sense his greasy, filthy fingers that rubbed off on it.

There was no way I was going to touch that, never mind eat it.

It'd rather starve.

And with that, I lit the diseased thing on fire.

I was left with just my precious camomile tea to get me through the rest of the day.

The last lesson of the day was over with, and I dismissed the students from class.

I was the last to leave as I packed up a few things and cleaned off the whiteboard.

Outside the back of the building, there was my beautiful Aston waiting for me.

I tossed my satchel in the back before I got in and started the engine.

Roaring away as usual.

My usual journey home was interrupted that day as I witnessed Miles once again being beaten up by other students.

He was getting hurt, badly.

I put my foot down and headed straight towards the crowd.

The kids didn't stop, but then neither did I.

I was only three yards away when the students finally realised I would knock them down.

They scattered and I pushed my foot down on the brakes and jolted the steering wheel to the side so I wouldn't hit Miles.

The car came to a halt, and I leaned over, pushing open the passenger door; Miles was on the ground by the car.

"Get in," I told him.

Miles was pretty beaten up, but he didn't want to go home, and frankly, I was still hungry.

He suggested a place and gave me directions.

It looked like a fifties American diner but was clearly going to be the opposite inside, with British teens as staff and saying the food is American just because it's of larger portions and would be covered in cheese.

It wouldn't be to my taste.

I'm more of a simple cheese and cracker type, but it's where Miles suggested so I wasn't going to say no.

We sat at a booth near the back and sat opposite each other. I was facing the window towards the car park, half five in the evening and already it was nearly pitch-black outside.

I tended to Miles' wounds.

I had a first aid kit in my satchel, which the boy seemed to find amusing as I told him and cleaned the blood off his face.

It was after this a waiter came towards the booth, and strangely Miles was happy to see him.

"Billy!" He smiled.

What?

"What are you doing here?" This Billy fellow seemed pleased as well.

They continued their catch-up while I sat there seething. I was wasting precious time.

"How's Max?" Miles glimmered.

"He's in the back."

I finally stepped in. "Is he the chef?"

It seemed like a simple question, but it left both of them in laughter.

"Nah, he's my dog."

Disgusting.

"You keep your dog in the kitchen?"

"Yeah, you wanna see him?"

The man seemed to misunderstand my signals regarding the canine. I simply said no.

At that point, the waiter, who unfortunately knew Miles, finally asked who I was.

"Oh! Right, sorry. This is Professor Valentine," Miles answered.

"You're dining out with your professor?" Billy asked. I knew he would, it did look odd for a normal person.

"I suppose." Miles shrugged. "He helped me with an issue at uni and he was hungry, so we came here." The boy spoke quickly; I'm surprised I could keep up, never mind Billy.

"Some kids were giving him trouble on his way home."

"What?" Billy's face sank. "Again?"

"I'm okay. Valentine got there before any real damage was done."

Billy then looked at me. He thanked me for helping Miles.

I didn't know this Billy, but I wasn't too fond. There was something off about him to me.

But finally, he took our orders and was off back to the kitchen.
"Who is that?" I asked Miles.

He apologised for the whole thing and told me it was an old childhood friend. I didn't trust the man, but I nodded and smiled along as Miles talked to try to seem interested.
Luckily, this Billy understood some table manners and left straight after serving our meals and thank goodness too because I was starving.

The food was salty and greasy, frankly too much for even a dozen people to consume but I was too hungry to complain.

It was after we had both eaten that I got to really talk with Miles. It was the first time we talked away from the university grounds and quite frankly he was a different person. He's usually so timid and keeps to himself, but out in the real world he seemed so open, he was a free soul.

A free soul for me to capture.

We talked well into the night; I even got a few laughs out of him, and honestly, he did with me too.

Most of the night my eyes were fixed on Miles.

Until at one moment, they drifted elsewhere.

Behind Miles, I saw a glimmer of red.

I looked in the direction of the light outside the window, and there the dreaded crow and Dobermann were staring at me with their sinful eyes.

Why were they following me?

I always completed my missions with no issues.

They knew something I didn't.

Miles noticed I was distracted and asked if I was okay.

"Huh?" I felt I was in a trance looking at those demons. After looking back at Miles, I now saw Nuntius and Perfidus had vanished. "Sorry, I thought I saw something." I let out a light chuckle, clearing the air. "What were we talking about?"

We went on for hours more until the diner itself was closing and we were told to leave.

I had offered Miles a lift home. The drive was silent but peaceful. It was a sort of comfortable silence you only get with people you've known and trusted for years.

It was odd to me.

Miles thanked me for helping him and for spending the evening with him before he left the car and headed towards the student accommodation.

I sat there and watched him, the Aston purring away around me.

It was strange.

In all my years, I had never met anyone like Miles Green.

10
Miles

Everything from that day forth changed for me. Every day, week and month, things were running smoother. I put my trust into Valentine's hands, and I didn't regret it one bit. Why would I? The man had somehow caused miracles in my life. I was able to go to university at the normal time, attend class and get home without worrying about Joe or any other students teasing me. They all left me alone, didn't even acknowledge me. I know not everyone enjoys it, but I felt truly free to be invisible to everyone. It was just me and Valentine against the world.

I had no idea why the man took such a liking to me, but something had me guessing that I reminded him of himself. I could tell by the way he always looked at me with those intense dark-brown eyes, as if he was reaching out into his past, hoping to change his fate. If his business with me was simply to help a student, a friendship or much more, I didn't care. He was intoxicating and I wanted every piece of him.

One Saturday while it was bucketing down with rain outside, the sky overtaken by grey clouds, I remained in bed for most of the day. I snuggled into the pillows, hot coffee in my hands, warming my frozen fingertips. The heating in this building was poor but luckily, I had enough blankets to keep myself toasty warm. That, and the fact my laptop was overheating on my lap. It had only been twenty-four hours since I last saw Valentine and yet I already felt myself yearning for him. It remained mild for a while, as I distracted myself with Netflix shows, it was just a small nagging feeling in the back of my mind. But as I grew tired of staring at a screen, the feeling swelled until I felt like I was going to burst into tears. I had to do something to channel this feeling before I exploded.

I reached over the side of the bed and rustled in my bag until I found my sketchbook and pulled it out. I grabbed my pencil and turned to a new page before I let the feelings flood out of me and spill onto the paper. His chiselled cheekbones, his lonely lips, ancient eyes. His very presence that silenced the room. I hadn't been aware that I was crying while I sketched him until a teardrop landed on my hand. I sat back and gazed upon the man's likeness on the page. My tears soon dried up as this lead version of him comforted me. The comfort that on any of these lonely, rainy days, I still had a piece of him here with me.

The following day I didn't wake until gone twelve. I had planned to have breakfast with Billy that morning. My absence worried him, and I could hear him knocking on the door as I retreated from my slumber.

"Just a second," I groaned tiredly. I was still half asleep. I stretched out my arms and legs so far that my whole body pulsed with satisfaction. I slowly sat up as I rubbed the sleep out of my eyes. I rubbed too hard, and my vision was fuzzy momentarily before everything came into view again. I turned to my bedside table and yelped to see Billy there.

"I didn't say you could come in!"

I frowned.

"I was worried." He sighed as he looked down at me. "You're never late."

"I wanted to sleep in." I didn't want to explain any further.

He frowned. "You could've told me." His eyes wandered over to my sketchbook and picked it up before he started to flick through the pages. "Y'know, you've been acting weird ever since you started hanging around—" He got to the sketch of Valentine. He turned the page to me and pointed at it. "Him."

"I don't know what you're talking about." I got out of bed, blanket still wrapped around me. I did know, ever since I got closer to Valentine, I barely spent any time with Billy. Not on purpose, it was just Valentine was on my mind so much lately that it was hard to think of anything else.

"I think you're very much aware of what I'm talking about."

He followed me, sketchbook still in his hand. He gestured with it as if it were a part of him as he lectured me.

"It's not safe spending your personal time with your teacher, Miles."

"Why?" I knew where he was going with this, but I remained calm as I shuffled into the kitchen with my blanket, getting myself a canned drink from the fridge and cracking it open.

"Miles, you're sketching him. You clearly have a crush on him, that's fair enough." He sighed. "But you can't keep hanging out with him; you could both get into serious trouble."

"I'm not a child."

"That's not the point." Billy pinched the bridge of his nose with his fingers, he took a pause before he looked back to me finally. "You just... You need to keep quiet about this. You'll only make a fool of yourself if you tell him how you feel."

I looked at him with a blank expression.

"So you want me to be miserable?"

"I want you to be safe. Please, just stop spending time outside of uni with him. It's a crush, it'll pass."

I huffed as I slumped down on the sofa.

"Fine." I didn't meet Billy's eyes as I replied, "If that'll make you stop wittering on."

11
Dolor

It was April, a few weeks before the university's Easter break.

At this point, my morning usually consisted of meeting Miles in the staff car park, and then we'd walk to class together.

However, the past week he had not met me before lesson, nor did he wait for me after or want me to join him at lunch.

Odd.

I remained calm about the situation; I wouldn't get anywhere if I forced myself upon him. He had to come to me.

I got out of the car and headed towards the back entrance when, by my absolute surprise and annoyance, I saw Miles walking towards the university, with Billy.

That lowlife.

Billy was up to something.

It's only been since he's known about me that he's been hanging around Miles a lot more.

I don't know what he was planning, but I didn't like it.

It was corrupting my mission.

Soon they were out of sight, and I made my way into the department.

I headed straight to the lecture room; no one was in there yet.

After closing the door behind me, my eyes locked onto Miles' desk. A pile of work still upon it.

I walked the steep steps and shuffled between the desk and chair to sit down.

I rooted through endless pieces of paper and books that were of no use to me. Nothing personal that would give me a clue about why he was avoiding me.

At last, I got to the bottom of the pile. Hidden underneath all that paperwork seemed to be a sketchbook.

I didn't know Miles was an artist.

My curiosity was strong, and I had to open it.

It was captivating.

I was one for art and Miles sure had talent.

There were endless sketches of flowers, trees, grey squirrels, ravens. There was an incredibly detailed sketch of Pellew Island Beach in Jamaica.

I could envision the waves moving, the sea hurtling into itself.

I turned the page and clenched my teeth slightly at a very well-drawn but hideous-looking beast: a dog.

I imagined it was Billy's dog.

What was it again?

Dex?

Dash?

Jax?

Mack?

Max!

Stupid-looking thing with its tongue flopped out and its droopy eyes.

I suspected Miles drew things that made him happy.

I quickly flicked away from that fleabag page.

And soon enough, my dark heart sank.

He drew… Me.

I felt overjoyed to know the mission was moving forward, that it was a success.

But as I looked at that drawing, I could pinpoint each pencil stroke. I could see the care he'd put into it.

I had never known anyone to do such a thing for me.

It made my heart burn.

I felt a deep sorrow inside.

After all my years, both living and dead, this was the first time I truly felt wanted.

The bell rang.

I hurriedly put back the sketchbook and everything else back on top.

Just as I was walking down to the front of the room, students were entering.

A close call.

Miles was the last to walk in after everyone else was already sat down.

But he didn't greet me.

He didn't even look in my direction.

Billy was to blame; I knew he was.

He was messing with me, with my mission.

I didn't show my anger about it though. That would've just made things worse.

I went on with the lesson as if I were any other professor.

I wouldn't have this one slip-up ruin everything.

I tried to make out that Miles ignoring me didn't bother me.

That in fact, I didn't care.

Mainly because I really didn't.

But also, if Miles saw his distance from me didn't affect me, he would come rushing back in no time.

And something of the sort did seem to happen.

Throughout the day, Miles' silence turned more to sadness.

I could tell at lunch when I didn't sit with him. Usually I waited for him at lunch, and he was the one to walk right past without a glance. Now, it was my turn. His shoulders were low and faced towards the table as I strolled past.

He was the same during the last lesson.

What had Billy said to him in the first place?

It wasn't good.

And I feared my entire afterlife was at risk if Miles didn't bounce back to me soon.

At last, the bell ending the day sounded.

I wished everyone a good weekend and then followed with, "Miles, can you stay behind for a moment, please."

I could feel that the students sensed tension, that maybe Miles was in big trouble.

If anything, it was the complete opposite.

Everyone left.

Miles stayed stood by the side of his desk, so I approached.

I leaned my hand against the desk and looked into his eyes while he kept his gaze to the ground.

He was hiding something within himself.

"Is everything all right?" I asked.

There was no response.

So I continued. "I saw you with Billy this morning, did he upset you?"

Miles said no.

"But he said something, right? To make you like this?"

"I suppose," Miles admitted.

I knew it!

Billy, that piece of shit.

I was furious, some complete stranger was jeopardising my entire operation. I tried my best to mask my fury, the fire in my eyes coated with fake softness. "What did he say?"

Again, Miles was silent.

I had a feeling that, whatever Billy had said, it was directed at me.

There was a stillness in the air; it was strangely comfortable, and it was easy to see Miles found it to be the same.

He had a secret he so desperately wanted to tell that was locked up inside him.

I had hoped I knew what that secret was.

So I did my best to help usher Miles to tell it.

Gently, I slid the paperwork on his desk to the side till I got to the sketchbook.

"You know, I never knew you were so talented at art."

Miles' eyes grew wider, nerves painted in them.

I opened the sketchbook and made my way through the pages for the second time.

"I'm rather fond of them," I added. "I imagine you draw the things that you like."

I got to the last page.

"Am I right?"

I slowly turned the drawing into Miles' view.

Silence.

I kept my eyes on Miles; he kept his eyes on the drawing—seeming to be unable to look up at the real thing.

Perhaps I was wrong?

Thousands of situations were rushing through my head concerning what was going on inside Miles'.

I felt I had failed.

Failed myself, failed my master.

I would be banished and become one of those snotty nosed angels.

Doomed, I was! Doomed!

Yet, as all this torturous misery was going through my mind, two options were tossing through Miles'.

Do I, or don't I?

I could see the inner battle Miles was going through still as I was distracted by my own torment.

All that ended soon after, however. As Miles chose 'I do.'

I was surprised to find that Miles took no time in kissing me.

It was no peck; it was slow and sweet.

It meant something to him.

I admit it was something special that caused my eyes to close and my arms to make their way around Miles' waist. His lips were soft and delicate. It was something I had never experienced in all my years.

It felt as if time itself had slowed; all there was was that moment.

After Miles had made his feelings obviously clear, he was honest with me.

He told the truth; that Billy told him to contain his feelings, to oppress them.

I knew Billy was trouble!

That scoundrel.

But no matter, because now my operation was in full swing.

I had tricked Miles into loving me.

All I had to do now was woo him with my incredible charm and romance.

It would only be a matter of time until Miles' soul was mine.

Step Five of being successful as the Demon of Heartache and Pain: Have the victim fall utterly in love with you.

That evening, Miles came back to mine.

The ride back was quiet, but comfortable.

As the tender sound of a guitar played through the Aston's speakers softly, Miles sat in the passenger seat. He looked timid, his legs glued together, and his hands linked; it seemed understandable that he'd be nervous.

He still managed to appreciate the car though which I very much enjoyed. He mentioned his love for classic sports cars; it felt like fate that I got the Aston all those years ago to lead up to this moment.

The sky was pitch-black when we arrived at the manor.

Only the front of the building could be seen by the outdoor porch lights, the rest was covered in a dark mist of the night.

Despite the ominous look of the place, Miles seemed comfortable enough to get out the car with me.

He became distracted by the manor, by its giant presence in the countryside.

However, my attention was drawn behind me at the time.

I could see headlights in the distance, not moving.

For a moment I believed I was followed, that someone other than Nuntius and Perfidus was spying on me, but moments later those same headlights disappeared.

Turned off.

Maybe one of the locals, I thought.

Inside, I was sure to make the place look and feel much more homely.

Miles slowly walked into the main hall before I turned on the lights, but when I had, I could hear an astonished 'Wow' come from him.

Revealed to him was a wide, colossal room with enormous arched windows and wooden panel floors. The lights gave a warm glow to the otherwise monstrous hall. Although the spiral staircase with its detailed wooden banister gave a Victorian charm to the place.

Miles asked, "You live here?"

"I sure do." I grinned at the thought of how little it took to impress him. "Drink?"

Miles declined. He may have been a fool for falling for the demon who would crush his soul, but he was sensible in the sense of knowing when it's appropriate to be intoxicated.

I, on the other hand, needed alcohol to get through the ludicrous night that was to unravel before me.

I led the boy into the lounge where the fireplace was already lit and slowly burning away; the sweet noise of a crackling fire echoed up the chimney as Miles got himself comfortable on the sofa, a two-seater with cotton stitching, laced with black and crimson, two plump cushions perched on either side.

Miles was quiet as I got myself a drink. I stood with my back to him at the drinks cabinet as I poured myself a glass of Haig Dimple's Royal Decanter whisky.

I sat.

At first, there was stillness between us.

I imagined Miles felt awkward, or perhaps he was engulfed by the moment.

I managed to start a conversation with the boy.

I thought we'd start light. We began with just discussing the university, how Miles felt with it being his last year. He seemed relieved at the thought of not going back to that place.

He asked when I decided to become a professor.

A tough area to discuss but I managed to make something up.

"My father was a professor," I lied. "An excellent one, at that." I went on, saying how the old brute had inspired me to teach.

In truth, that codger taught me nothing more than hatred and pain.

Nevertheless, my lies seemed to be getting through to Miles.

He could see some humanity within me.

Miles continued to ask me questions about myself and honestly, I'd soon had enough of it. Usually, I love going on and on about myself, but his questions were exhausting.

I wanted to know about him.

When we're given our missions, we're told very little of the victim.

All I was told of Miles was where he attended university, his age and sexuality.

The rest was up to me.

I asked about his childhood, his parents.

"I grew up in London," he began. "On Bermondsey Street with my mum and dad."

He seemed down talking about it; I asked him to carry on, hoping he'd reveal something.

"We were happy," Miles started, indicating soon that they were very much the opposite.

He went on to tell me that he came out to his parents when he was seventeen, and although they were supportive, things weren't the same. "They just saw me as a label," is what he said. He was no longer Miles, their son. He was simply 'their gay kid'.

I almost felt sorry for the lad that his own parents couldn't see past his sexuality. They believed he fancied every male around his age.

He went on to tell me he had a young sister, Holly, who was only born a year before he left for university.

His face dropped further; he believed his sister was a sign of his parents starting again, trying to bring up a 'normal' child.

I cringed at the word.

I never understood it. What was normal? Nothing more than a bunch of ignorant people who believed they knew what was right. But in fact, it was only what was right for them.

"I haven't talked to them since I moved away," Miles admitted.

His whole three years at university, nothing from his parents. No text, call, no birthday, or Christmas card.

He mentioned that when it's half-term, he spends the holidays with Billy. He has never dared to go back home.

Billy, I thought.

I wanted to know more about him.

I asked: "When did you meet Billy?"

"It was at summer camp," Miles said. "I was all alone; I struggled to make friends," he admitted. "Soon as we met though, we just clicked." He paused, seeming to recollect the memory. "I was about eight, I think. Been friends with him ever since."

I asked how old Billy was, what he was like. I wanted to know as much as I could about this man who seemed to be purposely sabotaging my mission. But Miles simply said, "He hasn't changed one bit."

At the time I was too intoxicated to understand what that meant.

But now, of course, it's crystal clear why this Billy seemed so against me, so determined to protect Miles from me.

My mission was well on its way now, though. Nothing could stop me.

As the night went on and the alcohol began to influence my mood further, Miles eventually gave in to wanting some for himself.

From there onwards our conversations were a lot lighter, there was a constant giggle within Miles as he talked.

We talked of past embarrassing moments; some of mine were even real.

We laughed, sometimes to tears.

And we both felt in good company as the fire roared on, wrapping us both in its warmth.

I wanted to take things further.

Although it was warming Miles up to me even more, friends could be doing this. Even strangers could sit by a fire, get drunk and laugh together.

I needed to add romance.

I needed Miles to feel suffocated without my love.

I stood. I had already drained a lot of the alcohol out of my body so there was no stumbling around.

I made my way over to the record player.

My usual classics wouldn't do. Too sharp.

I managed to find something with a gentler tone and placed the vinyl down on the platter mat and lifted the tonearm. The vinyl slowly started to spin, a slight scratching sound coming from the speakers.

Delicately, I let the stylus press against the vinyl, and soon the sweet sounds of a low violin and piano began to dance out the speakers and within the air.

I turned; Miles still looked quite nervous despite the amount he'd had to drink.

I approached him and offered my hand, "Would you care to have this dance with me?"

I wasn't the best dancer in my time, but in this modern age with all these strange dance moves, I'd say my classic style would seem professional to many.

The boy was hesitant at first; I imagined he probably didn't want to embarrass himself.

Nevertheless, the alcohol helped me on that front: it had influenced him to take my hand and stand.

We walked to the centre of the room, where no chairs could get in the way.

Miles didn't seem to know what to do, so I guided him. I placed both his hands on my shoulders before I placed my own on his waist.

The music guided us across the floor, the violins strong current and pianos light embrace flowed along with us. We were nothing more than two simple flowers caught up in a river.

The boy couldn't keep his eyes off me, and vice versa, for that matter.

How did a mere five minutes feel like an eternity with him?

And I strongly believe my decision to do this had worked, romance was there. It was in the music, in the air, in his eyes.

Now I hadn't just made him fall for me, but I had completely swept him off his feet.

I stood corrected as Miles kissed me once more. But this time it didn't feel rushed, that he didn't feel a great deal of anxiety when doing it. It was slow, delicate. It was a kiss I had like none other before.

It was that following morning I arose to the sight of Miles beside me.

Even asleep he was gentle.

Breaths were deep but quiet.

And no, nothing happened. You're all a bunch of dirty minded, blithering idiots.

To your surprise, I have never gone that far with any victim.

Frankly, it was against my job's rules and better yet, the act had nothing to do with falling in love from Hell's point of view.

I couldn't recollect too well what happened the night before, but there was an indication we both passed out. We were both still clothed in yesterday's garments and Miles seemed tuckered out completely.

As I lay there, my eyes rested upon the boy.

There are many others who may have felt glee and a sense of calm looking upon their resting beloved, I simply felt nothing.

Better yet there was a sense of emptiness of where a heart should be but never was.

But even that was the first time I had that feeling.

I used to enjoy the feeling of coldness within these fake relationships, but here I felt I should feel something. I should.

There was a sorrow deep inside me that wondered why I was so incapable of feeling love.

I could no longer lie there in pity.

I would continue with my mission, making my affection as convincing as possible to the boy.

I embarked my way down the grand stairs to the kitchen.

I had no idea what Miles liked, but if he was able to eat the slop they serve at university, then anything I'd make would most likely be edible.

I decided a simple Monte Cristo would suffice.

Yes, maybe not the quickest of breakfast recipes to make, but I wasn't going to make any old crap.

I wouldn't deign to make my eyes look at such peasant alternatives.

It was almost therapeutic to make as I laid out slices of bread and neatly grated the mature cheddar over each.

I found myself humming, which was odd.

I laid the finely cut ham upon the cheese.

A third slice of bread was slathered with a rich mayonnaise, before I sandwiched it between the other two.

I positioned a pan over the lit flame on the stove, the metal lightly covered in olive oil. Both sides of the sandwich were painted with a mixture of egg and melted butter.

There was time to spare as the bread toasted away in the pan, so I decided to make myself one of my scrumptious camomile teas.

The water boiled as I flipped the sandwich over in the pan.

The bread turned to toast as I stirred the tea leaves in with the boiling water.

The tea was left to brew as I tossed the sandwich over one last time until it was golden brown in colour.

With the stove off, I placed my glorious Monte Cristo creation on a plate for Miles.

At last, I was content as I was alone once again with my favourite thing on this planet.

My eyes closed as I took the first sip of the sweet tea.

A moment of pure bliss that was short-lived as a stampede seemed to be making its way down the stairs.

Miles stood before me looking flustered.

"It's ten to nine!" he exclaimed.

I didn't respond, my face poker until I clocked that it was Friday, and that meant we were was going to be incredibly late for university.

If Miles hadn't known the time, I could've turned it back.

But he did know, and me changing the time would only make him more suspicious.

After all this time he was still in disbelief about how I fixed his books; they were practically in brand-new condition after I mended them—a mistake on my part.

I was sure to show I was very much ordinary.

Miles expressed his concern with being late.

"We have to go!" he said worriedly and scuttled out of the kitchen.

"Wait!" I called out. "I made you breakfast."

The boy ran back in and grabbed the Monte Cristo that I had taken precious time and effort making. He sank his teeth in, running back off as he did so.

Oh, why did I have to be stuck with a millennial?

I took one last sip of the camomile tea before I had to go, leaving the rest to go cold. I could've cried at not being able to finish such a delightful hot beverage.

I joined Miles outside where he waited by the Aston.

He asked if I was okay with driving him to university.

I didn't object.

We were approximately thirty-five minutes late when I had finally parked the Aston, surrounded by all the other professors' hideous Vauxhall Astras, Renault Clios and Skoda Fabias, all of them a tasteless grey or maroon.

I felt truly sorry to leave the Aston surrounded by around such dreary sights.

I suggested Miles didn't attend class until after lunch, so no suspicions were raised.

The boy agreed and he went on to spend that morning in the library as he used to long ago.

I went to class as usual.

As I entered, I was met with all the students in the middle of a war, it seemed.

There was shouting and pushing, paper balls being thrown around the room, desks knocked over.

I had never known a group of young adults to be such imbeciles.

How the human race had devolved.

"Enough!" I exclaimed, and everyone came to a halt.

After I had the students clean up their mess and got them seated, they decided it was my fault such a scene had unveiled.

I was simply astonished they had the nerve to say such a thing to me, as though they were simply incapable of waiting.

Humanity was truly doomed.

They went on to ask where I had been, what took me so long.

I simply told them I had some errands to run and that quite frankly it was none of their business.

"Do you see me making you divulge your morning routine to the class?"

Everyone stayed quiet after that remark, and I went on to teach the rascals something their ape-like brains would clearly forget within seconds.

It honestly felt odd how normal that day seemed after such a strange start.

At lunch, I found myself seated with Miles as normal, and no one raised any concern.

Either the university was stupid or no one in the damn place communicated to note that the time I entered the classroom and Miles entered the library was almost the exact same time.

But nothing. There I was sitting with the student I had previously spent the night with, and everyone presumed it was another innocent discussion-filled lunch on literature and history.

The only history talk that went on was about last night.

Miles asked if anything happened.

I comforted him with a no; he seemed worried that we did and that somehow word would get out.

And despite the risks of last night, Miles said: "I would love to come again." If I didn't mind, he added.

"I would love that too," I replied. I made sure to smile at the boy and seem delighted to spend more personal time with him. In reality, I thought soon this cat-and-mouse chase would be over and I would return to Hell, where, despite the constant screaming and heat, I could get some rest.

Once lunch had ended, everyone returned to their classes, including Miles.

I was sure something depraved was afoot.

I could sense something was against my purpose of being there. There was a heaviness against my chest, my lungs felt as if they were caving in as I went on to teach.

I battled through it, but I could tell from everyone's faces they sensed something was wrong with me. Miles especially looked terribly worried as I broke into a cold sweat.

Lo and behold my nightmare came true as my sentence was cut off midway through. There was a knock at the thick wooden door and the large Headmaster Oxley peered into the room.

He wanted to have a word with me alone.

Maybe the staff in this place did communicate after all.

I had the students carry on with some reading while I attended to deal with the new problem.

Within the walls of the headmaster's office, Oxley practically ordered me to sit.

It made me feel like a rookie demon once more.

"Tea?" the old brute asked.

I looked to him; his hands gestured to the kettle and teacups.

"You got camomile?" I asked, my interest piqued.

The headmaster's face dropped, unimpressed.

"Then no." I sat back in the seat, folding one leg over the other, while Oxley struggled as he sat, his enormous stomach billowing over the chair's armrests.

The length of his moustache made it difficult for me to read his emotions, but he soon made them clear.

"It has been brought to my attention that you have become involved with one of the students."

My palms became sweaty; I tried to reduce it by rubbing my fingers slowly together.

The headmaster continued when I didn't respond. "An external source has informed me that you are in a romantic relationship with the young Mr Green."

Billy.

I immediately knew it was him.

He had always suspected me.

And I knew someone was following me last night. All that time, it was that goody-two-shoes Billy!

"Now you're a very well-educated man, and one of the best professors we've had. But unfortunately, the representation of this university comes first, and I will not be losing my job because of you."

The large mass of a man had to take a long breath before he continued; the poor walrus had worn himself out.

"I will be contacting the police to have this situation dealt with, and Miles' parents will be informed."

Oxley had finished, as though it would be that simple.

As if I wouldn't fight back.

"I'm afraid neither of those things will happen, Oxley."

I was calm. It unsettled him.

I stood; my eyes fixed on the headmaster as they glowed a deep red, similar to those of Nuntius and Perfidus who had then joined me.

Their dark, misty souls whisked into the room and remained on either side of me momentarily.

Is that why they had been keeping a close eye on me?

Had they been protecting me?

At that moment I wasn't to know for sure, but I was glad for them to do my dirty work.

The fat man was flabbergasted. His eyes darted frantically between the three of us until I simply had enough of his silent pleading.

"Dispose of him."

The demons wasted no time: their souls thinned to mere particles as they forced themselves through the headmaster's nostrils and mouth. Their pure evil was drowning him.

The man squealed like the pig he really was as Satan's henchmen were absorbing both his soul and body.

Even for me, the sight was ghastly.

The man was dripping in a cold sweat as his fat and flesh began to quiver and shrink. At first, it seemed he was becoming a man of average weight, but the troublesome pair didn't stop there. As bone became Oxley's key features and skin began to shrivel like a dried grape, his screams became nothing more than the last elongated exhale the man could manage before a skeleton was all that remained. Even then, the duo reduced that to ash which they took along with them as their misty forms swam through the air and out the tinted window.

I remained alone in the office, simply astonished that I could get away with such a thing: no one had come to investigate Oxley's screams.

Good for me, bad for him.

But even if someone did come, they wouldn't have been able to help.

They most likely would've met the same fate he did if they disturbed Nuntius and Perfidus during a kill.

It occurred to me at that moment that I now had full power over the university.

There was no headmaster, so, therefore, I put myself in charge—it only took one snap of my fingers to make every single staff member believe Oxley had abruptly retired and selected me as his replacement.

This job was too easy, too fun.

Now there was no higher authority.

Billy had no power, nowhere else to turn to try to ruin my mission.

I had full control.

As the last bell of the day had rung and I finished up on my topic on novels that broke the mould in the early twentieth century. I told them to research William Burroughs and his work for next week.

Everyone then left—no one questioned my meeting with Oxley earlier that day.

Except for Miles.

He stayed behind when everyone else had left for the evening.

The boy looked incredibly worried as he approached me.

"What happened?" he asked me. I had a feeling he was anxious that Oxley knew about us, that he was in trouble.

However, I kept him on his toes.

There was an exciting thrill watching him dance with worry.

"When?" is all I replied with.

"When you were called to Professor Oxley's office." He was becoming restless and after a long pause, I gave a proper answer. My amusement at his panic quickly died down.

"I have been promoted." I said with a wide grin, making it plausible that me becoming headmaster was a joyful surprise. It did indeed shock Miles, as he replied with an astounded *"What?"*

"The old boy's retired," I started. "He's put me in charge as the new headmaster. Can you believe it?"

Miles was genuinely delighted that I acquired such a position.

His merriment was expressed through a kiss, through a tight embrace, and through two words: "Let's celebrate!"

12
Dolor

It was pitch-black out as we lay beneath the stars.

Miles had given me directions to a small wood in which he often spent his alone time.

"It helps me clear my head," is what he said to me on our drive down.

It seemed quite far to me; there were miles on end of country lanes, and we passed a local college and two golf clubs on the way. But the boy expressed how the distance never bothered him as he travelled to the forest and back on his bicycle. It was a natural detox he needed and enjoyed getting away from his busy life in the city.

I had my jacket upon the grass for the two of us to lie on after we reached the highest point within the woods.

Below was the maze of trees and flowers, but up here there was a clearing, nothing but the black sky above us.

The Aston's headlights remained on, being the only light provided to us on the cold night.

There was luckily an old track through the wood for me to get my baby through; I was not leaving her behind.

It was muddy and rocky along the track that had now been overgrown with weeds and tree roots, which at times made me fear the safety of the Aston, but we all made it in one piece, nevertheless.

The two of us lay there with a calming silence between us, our eyes kept to the stars.

The only sound was coming from the car as I'd left on the radio at a respectable volume.

At moments our hands brushed against each other, it made the boy tense up at times with his fingers twirling in hesitation at what to do.

I decided to finally link my hand with his.

His palm was smooth, his skin soft, delicate. These were hands that worked no harder than turning the pages of a book.

As one song changed to the next through the Aston's speakers, I thought to ask him, why he had brought me here?

His reply was simple, but it clearly came from the heart. "Because I like you."

It was a phrase that came to mean nothing to me after hearing so many victims echo those words to me over the years.

'I like you' meant nothing more to me than 'you are my current muse'.

I would be nothing more than a phase in the boy's life.

I would be his lover, his heartbreaker, then nothing more but a memory. A painful reminder, a part of his past he wouldn't wish to look back on.

But as his eyes met mine at that moment, I saw a glint within his pupils that made me feel as if I were still staring at the stars themselves. I wanted to kiss him. Even though it wasn't necessary for any reason at all.

I convinced myself it was, however. Miles had offered me his heart; in return, I gave him my lips.

Sometimes actions are easier than words.

I couldn't bring myself to return his feelings, partly because those words would be false. Partly because there was a battle within me—mind against the heart— that found me realising if the words did come as truth to me, it would mean nothing. Soon all this would be over, so why bother with feelings at all when you know it will come to an end?

I would be free from this soon, is what I comforted myself with.

Despite never having these strange feelings of such confusion before, I was convinced it was nothing. Just a shadow of old human affections I had never possessed.

I soon took my gaze back to the sky, my hands found themselves resting between the back of my head and the ground.

Even then, regardless of my best efforts to put some distance between myself and Miles, to obtain the same boundaries physically and mentally, the boy had moved himself closer and rested his petite head upon my chest.

He had to be the clingiest victim I had ever been involved with.

Whenever we were alone together since our first kiss, he required attention, and without even thinking I had given it to him.

Including that exact moment as I peered down and found my fingers entwined within the boy's dark curls.

I rolled my eyes at myself and took back control of my hand.

My mind and body were not in line.

Another silence had grown between us.

For Miles, I believe one of peace.

But for me, I simply wasn't talking because I was occupied with an argument within my own mind.

I was interrupted when Miles turned himself over, his chin rested upon his hands which leaned against my ribs.

"I want to take you somewhere."

I already thought this was the place he wanted to take me, but clearly, he had more planned.

I checked my watch: 11.37 p.m.

"At this time?"

"It doesn't close till four, we'll be fine." The boy stood as he revealed this unusual information to me. "It's not too far from here."

What kind of place is open at such strange hours?

Miles offered his hand out to me, I took it. "Wouldn't you prefer going back to mine?" I asked. "Aren't you tired?"

"Not yet."

The boy was gleaming with excitement as we reached the destination.

We were on the outskirts of the city.

The streets were dimly lit with only a few streetlights, with faint orange bulbs scattered around by different rundown buildings.

This place didn't seem of any kind to have a celebration.

It certainly wasn't romantic.

I would've taken him to a theatre, a pebble beach, a stroll by a moonlit lake. He brought me to a serial killer's playground.

Typical youth.

The only place to park the Aston was at the side of the pavement and I was reluctant to leave her. Hesitant that someone would steal or scratch her.

"It'll be fine," Is what Miles said to me; I hadn't realised my fondness of the vehicle was so obvious.

I locked the car and left it; I wasn't going to go against Miles' word. He seemed strangely comfortable here and confident that everyone around was lovely, so there was no need to worry for the Aston.

Miles led me by the hand to a dark brick building that was projecting flamboyant booms in a rhythm. It sounded awfully loud in there and it was only worse when the boy opened the metal door with red paint peeling and cracking off its rusty edges.

Unlike the dreary exterior, the room inside was warm and vibrant.

I hated it.

Although the room was rather large, it still felt packed.

People were everywhere, breathing their filth on each other as they danced around like wild beasts.

There were simple low tables around the back left wall that had a hoard of plastic cups and bowls of foods and liquids.

He had brought me to a zoo.

The music was something my ears had never been exposed to before.

It repeated with staccato beats and bizarre electronic sounds that made my brain boil.

Miles kept hold of my hand as he dragged me through the sea of people. I kept my other hand firmly to my side; I wasn't having any strangers touch my pristine body.

The boy led me to the very front of where a small stage stood.

To my disappointment, as I looked up there stood my nemesis.

Billy.

He was the one responsible for the terrible noises coming out the speakers that were far too powerful for anyone to walk away from without their ears ringing.

Others stood behind him on the stage with instruments: guitar, keyboard, drums.

While Billy stood there, microphone in hand.

Angelus Canticum

And below him was Max, I presumed.

The beast was bulky with a heavy cream coat.

Its ears burned brown, as were the circles around its eyes.

Despite the loud noises and large numbers of people in the room, the dog was stationary. It just laid there.

It looked old, weary.

Maybe deaf.

The music died down momentarily. Billy kneeled down when he saw Miles and me. A stupid smile on his face.

He was resistant about acknowledging me, and I him.

The hostility between the two of us didn't seem to register in the boy's head, however, as soon after greeting his friend, Miles was pulling me around again.

We only left the side of the stage by a few more feet before Miles joined in with the outlandish dancing like everyone else soon as Billy had begun his next song.

It was an odd sight for a demon of my age.

There was no rhythm to his moves, no flow.

It was as if he was doing whatever his body pleased as the music built up.

I was stiff. A solid iceberg within the ocean, refusing to crumble.

The boy could see my discomfort and reached out his hand.

I took it, regrettably, and he pulled me closer to him before he continued.

He expected me to just join in with him.

As if he were a comfort to me.

I only managed to move my feet.

But it was coordinated, in rhythm.

A simple two-step.

I had never felt so uncomfortable, self-conscious.

My proximity to others made me tense.

I could feel Billy's eyes burning into the back of my head as he sang.

I feared I looked as strained as I felt; Miles wouldn't want to fall into the arms of one who couldn't even keep himself mentally stable in such a situation.

I could see myself at one remove; I began mocking myself.

I couldn't take it.

Nowhere I looked was I free.

Even with my eyes upon the boy, I felt my stomach twisting. His happiness at that moment was nothing but a burden to me, which I didn't want to be around.

I had to get away.

"You want a drink?" I leaned close to Miles' ear as I asked. The place was deafening, I was surprised the boy could hear me. But he nodded and smiled at me, one of glee. He saw this as me getting comfortable in the place—that if I would be willing to go alone to get him a drink, then that must mean I was contented.

Quite the opposite.

His smile just made me feel sick.

It was a smile that made him seem proud of me, or maybe proud of himself that I was relaxed in a place that was almost his second home.

This place clearly meant something to the boy.

He, after all, was more than at peace in the place; he knew the building like the back of his hand and had already greeted several others before and after we spoke to Billy.

I had never known this side to Miles that was so open and confident. He was the complete juxtaposition to himself at university.

The place must've really meant something to him.

I walked away.

My head spun as I pushed my way through the crowd of people.

I felt so unstable as I reached the buffet.

My hands were quivering.

Why had this boy made me feel so weak? So hopeless?

I was not my usual self at all.

No one! I repeat, *no one* made the great Lord Valentine feel such inferior emotions.

I would not have my aching heart unlocked.

I sustained myself; I was resistant. I would get myself a drink and stay in the corner until the boy was done with his flamboyant moves and we would leave immediately.

We could go back to my manor where I would end this.

This mission had already gone on long enough; I sensed the demon twins were becoming impatient.

I made impatience the reason for my recent feelings too.

The confusion, the vulnerability; all a result of being on earth too long. I was simply impatient.

The job would be finished tonight.

I scooped up some of the punch in one of the glass bowls into a plastic cup. The liquid sloshed around slightly as my hands still seemed unsteady.

I turned and suddenly found myself burning all over.

My eyes were fixed on Miles; I found something about him I had never seemed to notice before.

His smile made his entire body glow.

His hair was a luscious dark brown and each curl waved into the other as he danced. His moves were graceful, freeing. His comfort in his surroundings brought butterflies to my stomach.

His billowing sun-coloured shirt swayed along with him and complemented his slim figure beautifully.

I could feel, and for the first time, I wanted to.

I wanted to feel love.

I wanted to feel him again, his skin, his lips, which for months I hadn't given a second thought to.

Now it was all I wanted, and it made my heartburn.

All this time I had concealed my feelings for him, and for what? To protect myself? Love did hurt terribly. But it was a hurt I had been deprived of for centuries, and now before my eyes was the young man that longed for me as much as I did for him.

Miles was my camomile tea.

My body took control as it walked me back over to Miles.

Everyone else was now invisible to me.

It was just me, Miles and the warming sounds of a low guitar and upbeat bongos.

Miles came to a standstill as I stood before him and held out the drink to him.

He was gentle. His smile sweet and eyes loving.

His fingertips brushed against mine as he took the cup.

My eyes stayed on him; I don't remember blinking.

This made the young man's expression almost turn to concern as his lips left the cup. I didn't give him enough time to change his emotions however. Before he had enough time to fully read my expressions, I had already planted my lips on his.

I could hear the plastic cup hit the floor as Miles linked his arms together around my neck. I had surprised him, I believe.

I had surprised myself too.

Every kiss up till now had been out of necessity, or one that Miles gave.

I had been shallow, disinterested in every exchange we had, but Miles never seemed to mind—perhaps he thought I was inexperienced.

This was also our first kiss in the close presence of others.

We stood there, surrounded by many eyes that could've easily judged.

But everyone was just a blur; Miles was the only one in focus to me as I retracted from his sweetened lips.

It was clear my sudden passion towards him came to a shock to him.

But it was a shock that made his heart jump.

He looked up at me, his face buzzing with delight.

It was a look you only got from someone who was clearly utterly in love and simply couldn't hide the fact.

I knew because I had the exact expression on my face.

I settled his excitement as I rested his hands upon my shoulders delicately and went on to do the very thing I struggled to that entire night.

Let go.

All my judgements on myself had melted away.

My ice-cold heart was now hot lava.

My movements were liberating. Not in time with any beat or timing, but simply flowed with the thick sound of trumpets and bass.

I went wherever Miles led, his shoulders and hips swayed opposite to each other.

Despite our different styles, our movements went together seamlessly like a jigsaw.

I watched the young man up and down as I mimicked his moments now and then when I felt unsure about where to go next. I simply felt inspired by his grace, his gentleness.

One hundred and eighty-four years and Miles was the only one to ever make me feel so alive.

13
Miles

Valentine first insisted we go back to his to celebrate his promotion, but a day already confined within grand halls had left me exhausted and I desperately wanted to take him to the place I loved most.

"There's a quaint place up by Milton. I go there all the time," I ventured.

"The place by the river?" He glanced over at me as he drove.

I nodded, "You can see the whole of the city up on the hill." I continued to look at him as he didn't draw a response, torn on what to say. "It would mean a lot to me to go with you."

He looked to me once more and he instantly fell for the classic puppy eyes trick. Big, teary eyes, slight pout and he instantly gave in with a nod.

"All right. You'll have to give me directions though."

It was about forty minutes till the forest was in sight and already I felt more at peace. We hadn't spoken much on the drive down apart from when I had to give directions.

"Just this left here," was the last direction I had to give before a smile began to form on my lips.

"I come here at least once a week, it helps clear my head, you know? Forget about university and the city for a while."

"I can't remember the last time I spent any amount of time in nature." Valentine said, half-distracted by driving. There was a loud thud underneath the car as he proceeded to drive up a narrow dirt track.

"Shit."

"There is a car park. We could've walked up," I suggested but he shook his head.

"I'm not leaving the Aston behind."

I couldn't help but smile. I knew car lovers were overprotective when it came to the classics, but this? Valentine saw the car as a friend, or even family. He was a man who lived all alone in a massive manor, it was both heart-warming and saddening that his devotion had to be turned towards a machine from his years of solitude.

The car groaned up the muddy track, as did Valentine; cursing under his breath whenever a stubborn rock or tree branch gave the Aston's tyres a tough time. Eventually, we made it to the top, clear of all the twisting trees. Valentine immediately got out the car before he rested, face down on the bonnet, seemingly to give it a hug.

"Thank goodness!" He said, letting out a loud sigh of relief.

It made me laugh to see him such a way, as though he was thankful to have found his lost dog. I got out the car and gently patted his back as I walked by.

"C'mon," I chuckled. I went to sit down but he grabbed my arm, I didn't even hear him move from his car.

"Wait." His tone was almost sinister. I feared I had got myself into something terrible. But then he went on to remove his jacket and placed it on the ground. "There you go." He looked at me with a smile as he gestured for me to sit.

We sat leaning against each other for a while as the sky darkened before us, but as the stars continued to glimmer, my back was giving up on me and I had to lie down. Valentine didn't waste any time in lying down beside me; his cold hand brushing against mine left me without breath. I clearly tensed up so much that he noticed. He kept his eyes on me as he took a hold of my hand, lacing his fingers with my own. His skin against mine filled me with a buzz of both excitement and fear: what would become of us? Was this merely a fling for a man who didn't know where to turn, so projected himself upon a younger figment of himself? Or was it truly something more? A forbidden love that he would risk it all for. Although it was daunting where it all might lead, right here, right now, I had never felt so safe. Here, away from the rest of humankind, sharing the stars with the one person who makes me feel at peace with where I am in the world, not haunted by the past, not worried about the future. Just here. Now.

I had no idea how long we were out there for, although the cassette in the car's stereo had played through twice and Valentine was almost asleep as I looked over at him. I gently nudged him.

"I want to take you somewhere," I said as he turned to me

I did feel bad, Valentine looked tired, preoccupied with his thoughts as we walked into the club. But I was so excited to take him to the places that meant the most to me. I pulled him to the front of the stage where Billy had just finished a song and was prepping for the next. The atmosphere of the whole place changed at that moment. Both Valentine and Billy had been unusually quiet, and I couldn't help but think there was some tension between them. Had I caused this? And I so badly wanted them to get along. The longer we stood by him, the sharper the tension was getting, and I had to pull Valentine away as Billy started the next song; I wasn't one to try to force friendships to blossom.

I was in a whole new element here. I had a good mix between my alone and social time. Maybe unbalanced; I sure did spend a lot more time on my own either reading or just watching the world go by. But whenever I could, I'd build up the courage to come here and support Billy achieve his dreams.

"You want a drink?" Valentine spoke into my ear. I could just about hear him over the pulsating music. I looked to him with a smile and nodded. He seemed to be opening up to the idea of this place, especially as he briskly walked off amongst the sea of people towards the bar. Even I would have a tough time walking through that lot without feeling at least slightly uncomfortable.

I remained where I was, at least here I had enough space to free myself. I closed my eyes and let the music take me away. While it was the classical sort that allowed Valentine to open up; this, right now, was exactly what I needed. My arms felt cushioned by the air as they swayed back and forth. My feet tapped away to the beat of the drums; I could feel the stickiness of the dried alcohol on the wooden floor against the outer sole of my shoes. It didn't bother me though. I was drunk on sound; I could've gone on forever. But I felt a presence before me. I opened my eyes and instantly smiled when I saw Valentine back with my drink.

"Thank you." I gently took it from his hand and had a sip before I looked back to him. He was silent, staring at me the whole time.

"Are you all right?"

Before I could express my true concern for him, his lips were against mine, pulling me close to his body. The kiss was so sudden that I ended up dropping my drink and fell into his presence, letting my lips melt into his.

Before now, I worried about what our relationship meant to Valentine. A secret fling, most likely. But as we kissed in a room populated with people, all those doubts washed away.

He loved me; he didn't have to say it for me to know.

He pushed me against the bedroom door as our kiss heated. He didn't bother turning any lights on in the manor when we returned, and I'm glad; I didn't want to leave his side for a second. Luckily, the moon shone through the bedroom window bright enough that night for us to see what we were doing, or him at least. I didn't have a clue. It was my first time. He lifted me up and continued to hold me against the door as he worked at undressing us both. He knew I was nervous; I shivered, and my breathing hitched each time our bare skin touched. I wasn't ready when he pushed up inside me and I yelped, digging my nails into his back, and my head fell upon his shoulder. He moved for a while before he carried me over to the bed. We lay down; he wasted no time in thrusting inside me once he was on top of me. It hurt for a while, but my groans quickly turned to moans and I wrapped my legs around his waist to pull him closer to my body. The fact that even in bed he was such a gentleman was incredibly comforting, he made this alien pleasure a new familiar, something warm and loving that I could hold onto forever. I was beyond relaxed as I heard the soothing sound of his deep moans against my ear. Entwined with him, I felt at home. Our souls were now linked forever, and I was certain I could always call him mine.

14
Dolor

The sun had just emerged over the trees opposite the manor when I woke.

Miles lay beside me still fast asleep, his arm relaxed on my chest.

It was early in the morning, maybe three a.m. when we returned back to my abode. We were drunk on love as we barely got through the front door when our lips had united together once more.

I could feel my veins pulsing, my heart thumping within my chest.

My mind was completely occupied, all I could think about was Miles—how much I wanted him.

As I looked upon him that next morning, I was reminded of how special that night had been. I was still incredibly intoxicated on romance, my affection for Miles.

I had almost completely forgotten I was a demon as I lay there beside him, our exposed skin comforted by the soft cotton sheets and each other's warmth.

I wanted to stay in that moment forever.

It was a Saturday, and therefore we spent most of our time lounging about.

I was perfectly comfortable as I strolled into the kitchen that morning in my boxers and a black silk robe.

The marble flooring was like ice beneath my bare feet.

It felt as though all my senses had been enhanced.

Every colour before me had brightened.

Each scent had sweetened and intensified.

Every touch was delicate and precious.

I wasn't long into making my usual scrumptious camomile tea when I felt the arms of my new love wrap themselves around my waist. His head rested upon my back as he leaned against me.

It made me feel safe.

"G'morning," I said, my tone soft, unlike many other mornings where I didn't even want to say anything to him. As I thought back to those times, I couldn't believe how cold I had been, and how Miles didn't judge me once for it.

"Good morning, my Valentine," he grinned. "Please, call me David."

The young man was extremely giddy.

I imagined it was because of the sex.

It was only last night that Miles mentioned he was a virgin.

I honestly wasn't surprised, but I was also glad.

I was glad I would be his first.

I was glad Miles would remember me as the one who first gave him that feeling.

That he would always know it wasn't a whim or one-night stand, but a revelation of our love. That we were now truly bonded.

I only hoped I would also be his last.

Would that be possible?

Could I simply live by his side forever? Leave my demon life behind.

Would it be that simple?

I could only hope.

We spent the morning back in bed.

Our legs laced together as Miles rested.

I had my eyes buried in a good book while I sipped at my tea now and then.

It simply couldn't get better.

I couldn't believe how long it took for me to feel this way.

I wasted my life messing with people's hearts.

I wasted a lot of my afterlife doing the same thing on a much higher scale.

But maybe it was meant to be.

Maybe I was always destined to find Miles. To fall in love with him.

They say everyone has a soulmate; mine just happened to be born more than eighteen decades after me.

If I hadn't lived life the way I did, I never would've found him.

I didn't want to think of what my afterlife would be like without him now. I can't even recall how I lasted so long without him.

As the day went on and the sun turned from a mustard glow to a lemon yellow, we were both still very much at rest.

We had only moved from the bedroom to the lounge.

I was still very much enjoying my book. I had reclined in my armchair, my slender legs reached out, my feet resting upon the coffee table.

Miles was sitting opposite me on the sofa, his legs were almost up against his chest as he used his lap for his sketchbook to rest against.

He was completely in the zone; his tongue even did that typical sticky-out thing that happens when someone is concentrating.

I looked to him now and again whenever I turned a page. The sun was coming in the window through rays and glistened upon him.

His skin glowed, his hair softened to a more milk-chocolate colour.

He always brought a smile to my lips.

There was a silence between us, but it was one of peace and comfort.

It was the kind of silence you got with the one you trusted most, that even though you hadn't talked to each other in quite a few long minutes, you would feel comfortable to bring up a conversation, or that simply a glance of eye contact was enough to fill your soul with a life's worth of words.

It was during one of those glances that we gave each other that my eyes remained on his.

"What are you drawing?"

"Something beautiful," were the only words Miles responded with, but that's all he needed to say. His expression said far more.

Absolute fondness.

Was he proud of himself about how well he drew? Or was it that what he was drawing made him feel happy?

I imagined it could be both.

"A piece of scenery, perhaps?"

"The only scenery I care to see." He was toying with me, simply teasing me with his clever, brief comebacks and desirable, bold grin.

I asked if it was an animal he was drawing.

"The heart of one."

Was he drawing an actual animal heart, I thought? *Then which animal?*

The young man was brief again in his reply, "The best of them all." He seemed proud of how long he could keep me guessing.

We could've gone on for hours, teasing each other.

Gazing into each other's eyes.

His were gentle, loving. Like still pools that I simply wanted to dive into.

Swim within his spirit, his passions, his love for me.

To know how he felt, how he thought.

He was a love that made me unbelievably curious.

Yet, it was a moment short-lived.

Miles stood once a beeping sound seemed to be emitting from a small device he was holding.

He told me he needed to leave.

His tone made it clear he didn't want to. That he wished he could stay forever.

"I need to go and study for a few hours."

I had to seem to understand; I was still technically his professor in his eyes.

I agreed with him, and I wished him well to his journey to the library.

Our lips touched once more that late afternoon.

I made sure to embrace the feeling.

The feeling of his soft lips.

The sensation of his warm body against mine.

It was slightly unnerving to think about what I'd be without Miles now.

Even for a few hours.

Would the warmth within me thaw out?

Would all the bright colours become dull once more?

I couldn't be sure.

All I could do was embrace Miles within my arms for as long as I could until the young man finally said he really needed to go.

And with that, I let him go.

It was a few minutes after Miles had left. I finally closed the front door after watching him walk away.

Already the stillness in the manor was unsettling.

Such a big place for one demon to live.

It was lonely without Miles in it.

I slouched back into the lounge. For some reason it didn't feel so lifeless in there, it was as though I could still picture Miles happily sat on the sofa, laughing and drawing.

It was with that vision that my eyes were drawn to the coffee table where Miles' sketchbook lay.

He'd left it behind.

I took it in hand, and I once more admired all the pieces I had already seen, but now in a new light.

Even his work seemed to become enhanced as I looked upon it with my new eyes.

It was then I came across his new drawing.

It was another of me.

But this one seemed to melt my heart like already soft butter in a pan.

He had drawn my complete likeness as I had sat in the armchair earlier on.

I could visually see happiness, love.

I had never seen myself in such a way.

It made me feel juxtaposed to my current mood, as though I were looking into another plane.

I was the darkness, craving Miles' light. I didn't understand how I had managed to cope without him for all those decades.

All those joyous times with Miles, times I felt alive again, seemed to have happened to another me in some other life, some other time. As now only my sorrow remained, years' worth of pain and loneliness came flooding in all at once.

Who knew true love was such a wonderful but devastating thing?

Miles.

Someone who was stuck on my mind, even though he shouldn't be at all.

A demon may not and cannot love.

Was I an exception?

For my love for Miles was deafening. An aching within, a feeling that I longed for a second chance at human life, normal life in the many forms it took.

Miles was my normal.

Yet it was one thing I couldn't have.

As I looked back at that sketch, I knew the man in that drawing was one that could not remain.

For a demon I was, and a demon life was all I knew; the only one I knew how to live. What would become of me if I no longer had that status?

Truly, it terrified me to think of what would become of myself since my hardened exterior had been melted away by Miles' flame.

Yet I also loved it; I loved the pain of love, the bellowing deep inside that yearned for his touch.

Yet as my black heart burned for his love, I was reminded of who I was.

What I was.

Why I was here in the first place.

Beyond the inside of the manor, a giant swoop sounded outside on the front yard, a curtain of black mist masking the lounge window.

It vanished as quickly as it appeared, with the sun soon glistening its way through the glass once more.

The sudden change caught my attention, and I made my way over to the window, once again finding Nuntius and Perfidus just standing there, staring right through me with their piercing crimson eyes.

I sank down within my own thoughts.

They knew all this time.

They hadn't been protecting me; they had simply been keeping an eye on me to ensure I went through with the deed.

They always knew Miles would become my weakness.

It's time, I could tell that was what they were telling me as they glared.

They had enough of waiting around, enough of me wasting time.

But how could I?

How was I to break the heart of the one I loved most?

Once the pair knew I understood, they swept back into their animal forms. Nuntius flying off into the sky with Perfidus running after her in the same direction.

I was left all alone once again, now with the daunting thought of what I was going to do, and whatever my decision would be, it would always have a terrible consequence.

I chose nothing.

I refused to break Miles' heart, but I also came to despise myself as anything other than a demon.

I simply hid away.

Later that evening, I had the Aston hidden away, parked in the garage to the far right of the manor. I had never used it before. I always had her out on display.

But now my existence had to disappear, as though I was nothing but a sweet dream to Miles.

With the car hidden away in the cobwebbed garage, I returned inside. There, I had all the lights turned off: The outside porch light, the kitchen, lounge, hallways, bedrooms, bathrooms—all in darkness.

I was living within my own pity.

I did nothing but sit in that armchair, pondering on my own thoughts. My regrets, my wishes.

Even my doubts.

Demons don't have doubts, I thought.

They don't have regrets or wishes either.

What had I become? And why did it hurt so much to feel?

I sat there for hours, drowning in my own mind.

Until the sound of rustling came from the front yard.

The sound of rumbling gravel and squeaking brakes, the clicking of gears.

He knocked on the front door. I knew who. I could tell by the gentleness against the wood.

I remained seated.

It was guilt that kept me away from Miles.

Even if I no longer wanted to hurt him, how could I carry on knowing that was my original intention?

It was pure guilt. The guilt of simply not being good enough.

He deserved far more than the sinful soul I was.

I was tied to my regrets, my sorrow, my pain.

And even though Miles washed those feelings away while I was in his presence, I couldn't bear the thought of that darkness seeping out and drowning him in it.

No delicate, precious soul should be wrapped in the arms of a demon.

He knocked again, each gentle tap against the door made my darkened heart break further.

I could only imagine the distressing thoughts racing through his mind, the rapid beating of his heart.

Even in my absence, I was hurting him.

But perhaps this way, his heart would still be broken, my mission would be done, and I would go back to the misery of Hell, where I belong.

At least that way I wouldn't see the sadness on his face, the pain in his tears.

It was a coward's way out, yes.

But I couldn't bear seeing him hurt.

It was another few minutes till Miles returned to his bike.

The rustling sound of gravel beneath his feet as he walked away and brought his bicycle back up onto its wheels.

The clattering of the chains returned as he left.

I prepared myself for my return.

To be dragged back down to the depths of Hell, the burning of its furnaces.

I remained sitting there, however. I was puzzled about why.

Hadn't my sudden disappearance broken the young man's heart?

He may have been far stronger than I had assumed him to be.

Perhaps he had faith in me.

His love for me stronger than his doubts.

How I wish I had that strength.

On that following Monday, I didn't return to the university.

It was tempting for sure.

Enticing to go back and act like everything was okay. That I could be around Miles, embrace him, love him like all was well.

But I couldn't kid myself.

The truth would've broken through one way or another.

I lounged around for the entire day feeling sorry for myself.

I didn't even go to bed the night before, I simply remained on the sofa, soaking up the last I could of that last day with Miles until my recollection of the memory had become altered and faded by my own brain. At that point, even the lounge had become grey, another lonely room.

At some point, I managed to shuffle my way into the kitchen.

This would be the first time I would eat something since the dread had set in.

Not that I ate much, a few biscuits were all I could manage.

They were bland.

Everything was.

That's usually how it goes though, you get a taste of joy—a taste of pure happiness and love, for it to then be ripped away from you, leaving everything completely tasteless.

With a minuscule amount of food within me, I returned to the sofa where I spent the remainder of the day, dipping in and out of a light sleep.

I found myself having nightmares.

Odd, as demons were the ones to make nightmares, not have them.

It was the same nightmare every time I closed my eyes: I was being dragged back down to Hell, me crawling at the earth's surface as I tried my best to stay there. But every time I still ended up back down there. That's when I would always wake up.

Was I actually scared of going back?

It seemed maybe so, but I didn't know if it was because I had become to loathe the place, or because I couldn't stand the thought of being so far away from Miles.

But then again, maybe both.

I admit I had become soft.

Miles had warmed my heart so much that I gained a significant amount of humanity.

I didn't fit in Hell any more; I would be torn to shreds.

I awoke once more in the evening, but not by the disturbing events in the nightmare.

It was a knock at the door.

I remained frozen for a moment until I finally arose when there was a second knock.

I peered through the peephole of the front door and saw Miles standing there; he looked blue.

I had made him feel that way; it was me, my fault.

I wanted to slap myself, I would've if I knew it wouldn't have been audible.

"David?" Miles called out as he gently knocked once more. It was clear he was trying to keep himself together, to not cry. "Is everything all right?"

I wanted to go out there, to open that door and embrace the young man in his arms. "It is now you're here," is what I would've said.

But I didn't.

I just listened to him, listened to him say he missed me, that his day at university was incredibly lonely without me.

"I'm worried about you," he mumbled as he clearly doubted whether I was even in the house. I'm just talking to a door, is probably what he thought.

The last he said to me was that he wished me well, and an "I love you." The three words that tore me up inside.

"I love you too." I murmured underneath my breath as I watched Miles move from the door.

It was then, when I was sure he had left, that I did actually slap myself, hard.

It stung like hell.

But it hurt no more than my heart did every time

those last words of Miles ran through my brain.
    Those sweet yet bitter words.

I love you.

15
Miles

I was sickened to think of what happened to David as I sat there in the back of his class. The other students murmured around me, questioning where he was. He never showed up, neither did a substitute teacher. So, in the end everyone left, laughing amongst themselves that they got to skip class, but I remained seated, hoping he would come.

By the time it was lunch; my head was spinning. There was still no sign of him, and I couldn't bear to think that it was because of me. Had he got into trouble? I envisioned a teacher coming over to me and saying the police were here to see me. It made me feel sick to my stomach, the thought of him getting into trouble because of me, maybe someone leave his house, saw me kiss him, found my sketchbook in his living room. My mind was racing with all the possibilities of what could've happened, none of them I could've been certain about. All this worrying and he could possibly just be ill. Either way, I had to go see him again, I needed to make sure he was all right.

I plucked up the courage to go one evening after uni. There was still no sign of his car and all the lights were off. I didn't understand, was he out of town? Why wouldn't he tell me? Take me with him. I knocked on the door and called out his name but there was nothing, the silence cut me deep and I wanted to sob.

"I don't know if you can hear me, I don't know if you're even in there... I miss you. Nothing has been the same without you. Wherever I go, I look for you, but the only place I've found you is in my dreams." I choked up on my own words. "I'm worried about you."

I waited, for a voice, for a light to turn on, the door to open, but there was nothing. I sighed, "I love you," before I turned away, tears rolling out of my eyes. Where was he?

I felt more alone than ever without David there, his absence was like a knife through my heart. Although my evening routine was the same, a quick ready meal for dinner, sit on the sofa by the toasty radiator and watch television, cuddle up in bed with a book, everything felt different, out of place. I couldn't name the feeling. The feeling of love itself was all too new for me, to have it snatched away from so soon was torturous. A glimpse of a life I could never have. I didn't read much of my book that night, no words on those pages could help me, none of them were of comfort. I gently closed the pages together and held the book close to my chest as warm droplets fell from my eyes. Curling up into myself, I could do nothing but hope, plead that he would come back to me. I had never needed someone has much as I needed him.

It was soon to be graduation and still there was nothing from David, no message, or call, or a knock at the door. The university had finally got a substitute in for him, but that changed very little. No one learned anything without him; the students had listened to him because he terrified them. It made the corners of my lips curl up at the thought. I used to be that scared of him too. His dark clothes and intense stare brought a shiver down my spine, yet I warmed up to him the more he opened up to me. I still questioned why out of everyone he chose me. But then I suppose you can't choose who you fall in love with.

Despite our time apart, I had to try again. My heart yearned for him, he was the addiction I was craving, and I needed another dose. I knew I had left my sketchbook at his, that may have been intentional, a ploy for us to meet again. I never could've imagined it would be under these circumstances, however. Either way, that was my way in.

I rode up to the manor, panting softly from how much I worked my legs up the steep hill on the way there. I dismounted and leaned my bike against the wall. I stood in front of the door for a few moments, contemplating what I should say. The more I stood waiting, staring at that door, the more it began to take on a menacing shape. Its high windows sunk down into mocking eyes, its edged curves split off into arms, folding them in judgement. *What are you waiting for?*

I knocked on the door before my brain could process on doing so, I stammered on what to say, all I could get out was, "I don't know what's happened between us." Just speaking out about it caused me to well up, I had to close my eyes to stop tears from emerging. "But clearly it isn't good." I sighed. I didn't waste much more time on how I felt; he clearly wasn't in there, or if he was, he wasn't interested in what I had to say. "I was just wondering if I could have my sketchbook back. Then I promise I'll get out of your hair." Still, there was no sign of the man I loved. "I wish you were here. I really feel like I'm just talking to a door right now." I joked to myself; a tear fell as I chuckled, and I quickly wiped it with the back of my hand. "I miss you."

The door opened and there he stood, sketchbook in hand. There was a clear desperation in his eyes that told me he had been inside all along, avoiding me because he had to, more than he wanted to. I had dreamt of seeing his face again for so long that I was shocked to actually see it again; I could conjure up no words. I hated him for ignoring me all those times, making me look like a complete fool. The amount of shit I got from the other students saying that he was probably arrested because of me. I cried out and flung myself at him, letting out all my rage onto him until there was nothing left, and I just sobbed against his chest. As much as I did hate him for what he did, I needed him. I realised that only more so as I rested against him, his arms tightened around me and pulled me closer, I was safe again.

16
Miles

I wasn't one for formal occasions. It felt exposing to wear such fitted clothing. I stepped into my Oxfords and laced them up delicately; they almost cost as much as my student accommodation, I wasn't going to risk any damage to them. My jigsaw was complete, and I stood in front of the mirror, patting down my blazer. I scarcely say I could recognise myself. I lived my entire uni life in jeans and t-shirts two sizes too big and now here I stood in a cream grey suit that hugged my body. I looked important. I smiled and thought of myself as some big-time CEO, or a famous actor, or a lawyer maybe?

Billy waited for me outside, the engine of his relic of a car chugging away as I walked over.

"You're sure looking dapper," Billy grinned as I got in the car. "I'll be your chauffeur for the evening." "Oh shut up." I laughed and pushed Billy's shoulder playfully. His teasing did not cease as he drove on. He called me 'Sir' after everything he said and glanced at me with a smirk.

"That's quite enough." I got out the car as we pulled up outside the building. "Off with you, servant." I shut the door with a slam and chuckled.

The old motor spat smoke out of its exhaust and jolted before it pulled back off into the road and Billy was out of sight.

I climbed the high steps of the building and made my way inside. I was early but still other students and teachers were stood around drinking and talking in groups. I scanned the room; David wasn't here yet. I made my way over to the buffet, no one seemed to notice me, and I was thankful. I didn't need any remarks about how different I looked. I kept my head down as the anxiety rose through my body, filling every fibre of my being with dread as to the inevitable questions that would soon arise. Just as I thought I would burst into a fit of tears, there was a tap on my shoulder. I turned and David stood before me, handsome and gleaming. Every fear shrivelled away; back with my man, I was safe.

17
Dolor

Miles told me he would meet me at the university; he didn't need a ride.

It was later in the evening when I finally returned to that building I had been avoiding for so long.

Its thick brick walls were booming with the sound of more modern music and artificial coloured lights plastered upon its ancient walls. It was quite disgraceful to see, really.

Both the staff and public car park were completely packed with a strange array of vehicles that I wouldn't want the Aston near if there were a space free anyway.

I parked her further down the road, a quiet street where all the residents seemed to be having their lazy dinners in.

I made sure the doors were locked, twice, before I headed towards the monstrous building.

I was terribly nervous, and I couldn't understand why.

Miles already knew of my undying love for him but to show it in such a place was unnerving.

Yes, I had already clicked my fingers earlier that evening so that every other student and professor saw nothing wrong with the two of us being together.

It was the thought of me actually being there for him, I was truly giving in to him, showing how much he ruled over me that I would give up a quiet night in for him.

Yet, it was a feeling I was proud to own.

Nervous.

Butterflies in the stomach.

All incredible feelings when you're about to look upon your beloved once more.

There were plenty of students outside, smoking and laughing uncontrollably in groups.

They didn't seem bothered by my sudden return.

I simply glided past them and into the university's main hall where the celebration was taking place.

As I entered that room bustling of life, I was no longer Dolor—Demon of Heartache and Pain. I was David Valentine.

Reborn.

The man I should've been all along.

And despite the ludicrous volume of the music that caused the floor to thump, and the suffocation of the number of people in the place; I felt settled as my eyes fell upon Miles who was stood alone by the buffet.

I didn't recognise him at first.

He was wearing such an elegant suit that perfectly sculptured his form in a way I could not describe. As though it was intentionally made for him all this time.

I approached him and tapped him on the shoulder, he swiftly turned in my direction.

His eyes fell on mine, his face suddenly glimmering with happiness.

With that nothing else mattered.

"You look ravishing," Miles blurted out. He clearly seemed embarrassed after he said it, as though it was a thought meant to be kept locked away.

He was right though.

I had picked out my best outfit for the night; I wanted to look my best for him.

I had on my favourite navy Austin Reed single-breasted blazer, which I acquired back in the eighties during a mission. I only wore it on special occasions, which usually meant during the break-ups.

I loved the thrill of their pain.

But now I was wearing it for a completely different reason. And I was simply glad that Miles approved of it.

"Drink?" Miles asked, gazing at me with a devilish grin.

He knew how much I liked it when he did that. When he bit his lip and grinned at me like he was up to something terrible. It sent shivers down my spine.

I nodded.

He gave me his drink before he went to get himself another.

I felt uncomfortable in his absence, and even when he returned, I felt unsettled by the atmosphere we were in.

Billy's night club was bad enough, but the music here was even louder and there were hundreds more people.

"Do you want to go outside?" Miles looked concerned as he asked, I think he noticed how truly uncomfortable I was.

I nodded once again which led to him taking hold of my hand gently, lacing his fingers with mine as he walked with me away from the crowd.

He took me around the back of the university and out into the courtyard.

Each pillar had soft glowing fairy lights twirled around them.

As did the water fountain in the centre of the courtyard which was surrounded by low plants in a circle by the base.

We were the only ones there, and I was glad about that.

There was no better feeling than being alone with him.

We sat on one of the benches under the pillared beams facing the fountain.

We were silent, but it was peaceful, comforting.

While everyone else was inside, overcrowded and being deafened by the insanely loud music.

I had my place of zen.

Miles: my rock in a rough sea.

I rested against his side; my head fell upon his as I relaxed.

I felt vulnerable once again.

As though he were the one protecting me, even though he was hundreds of years younger.

He was the only one I ever felt comfortable being submissive around, and he never seemed to see it as a turn-off. He just allowed it to happen with his arms open wide to me for an embrace.

We must've sat there for at least twenty minutes, at times I felt myself drifting off to sleep.

The tranquillity came to an end though when Miles livened up as a new song started, the low tones of electric bass rumbling from the speakers.

"I love this song!" He was ecstatic. "Please can we dance?"

In any other situation I would've said no, big crowds simply make me sick.

But he looked so excited, so hopeful to share that song with me, that I ended up saying yes.

He pulled at my arm as we returned inside.

I had forgotten how hot it was in there, how harsh the blue and green spotlights were to my eyes.

It seemed even more crowded, even when Miles tried his best to take me to a spot that seemed less so. I still felt claustrophobic.

The music was like none I had heard before, a steady beat with echoes and sad tones.

Miles was rested, swaying with the music.

Everyone around us moved so slowly yet I couldn't focus on any of them.

My arms stuck to my sides as my eyes darted around the hall at all the people who appeared as blurs while my head spun.

Soon it wasn't just in my head, the whole room was spinning around at unsettling speeds that made me feel faint.

I most likely would've, but Miles steadied me.

My rock.

His hands cupped my cheeks as he stared into my eyes, making me focus on him.

It helped; it really did. The world slowed down and once again; he became the only thing in view.

His hands traced down my chest before he grabbed hold of my hands, pulling me closer to him, out of the way from anyone else.

I couldn't help but fall in love with him all over again as I watched him dance, just as I did those many moons ago.

Even in the most chaotic of places, he was so graceful, so calming to look at.

I simply admired him.

His moves were addicting.

His body was tasteful.

He was my belladonna.

He looked to me as the song kicked up into the chorus again. He noticed me staring and laughed.

He seemed charmed by my admiration of him.

His arms linked around my neck as he joined me in the dance.

The two of us were now moving as one.

Everyone, everything else around me was a distortion.

My entire focus on the angel before me.

His glimmering eyes, his dark-chocolate hair, his sweet smile; all inspired a better version of myself.

Every precious moment with him, I wished they would last forever.

But we remained until the last moments of the song as it returned to its simple bass and faded into nothing.

Its ending led to our kiss; nothing felt more right at that moment than his lips to mine.

The whole world froze as we connected.

Our lips parted but our bodies remained, my chin upon his shoulder as my arms snaked around him tightly.

I didn't want to let go.

But then again, I soon had to.

My gaze was drawn before me as a couple of students cleared out the way to reveal the sinister twins lingering there, in the middle of the dance floor.

They were just staring.

They were invisible to the rest of the world, like ghosts.

Students were able to walk right through them and feel nothing but a slight chill.

But they were there, plain as day.

And they were warning me now. One last warning. *End it.*

Their eyes were seeping out with the darkest red, that which had the resemblance of blood.

Thick, threatening.

Even the blackness of their mist seemed to be emitting a dark glow of crimson and mulberry.

They were furious with me.

No matter what I did now, it would result in my punishment.

I had already gone too far, so as I stood there, I thought, *May as well go all the way.*

I grabbed Miles' wrist.

"We have to go."

I didn't explain, I didn't reason with him as he looked puzzled at me, repeatedly asking *why?*

I dragged Miles along beside me out of the building, keeping a tight hold onto his wrist as I rushed down the street, keeping him close by my side.

"David, what is going on?" His tone became more serious, frightened by my sudden franticness.

We reached the Aston. Opening the passenger door, I got Miles to get in before I hurriedly shut the door and got myself behind the wheel.

He looked to me, his eyes wide with worry. "What's happening?"

I didn't respond, I simply planted my foot down on the accelerator, flooring it down the empty road.

That, I see now, was a terrible idea, as it only made Miles worry more.

He continued to question what was going on as we both panicked, both for very different reasons. He demanded me to tell him, but I didn't know what to answer with, I couldn't tell the truth and I couldn't come up with a reasonable lie.

I resulted in doing something I still feel bad for to this day; as Miles continued to talk in his panic, I took one of my hands off the steering wheel and snapped my fingers, making him slump back in the seat, unconscious.

It was the only thing I could think of doing until I could get him somewhere safe.

18
Miles

I awoke from the feeling of the sun's rays beating down on me. There was an unstable feeling within me as my eyes slowly opened, seeing nothing but a blur of blues. I sat up slowly, trying to steady myself but the swaying continued, a deafening mechanical rumble flooding my ears. It was only after I rubbed the sleep out my eyes that the open ocean was revealed before me: turquoise blue and glistening from the touch of the sun. The sky's night blues slowly transforming into a mix of deep purple and red.

"What are we doing out here?" Was the first of many questions I had for David, whom I could sense in my peripheral vision at the wheel of the boat. He did not answer me. I stood, having to steady myself. I didn't have sea legs; not once had I ever been on a boat. I made my way towards him.

"What is going on? Where did you get the boat? Is it yours?"

"It is," was all David answered with before he finally met my eyes. "You're cold. Go down into the cabin, there are plenty of blankets down there."

I wanted to yell; I wanted to demand an explanation, but I was tired and frozen. I made my way down into the cabin and the sudden change from the cold air to this toasty cocoon was intoxicating. I found the pile of blankets and tossed myself into them like a dog into water.

"We're here," David said.

I wasn't aware that I had fallen back asleep. My eyes opened and I was curled up in the captain's seat. I perched myself up to see a small island. It was my island, the one I always dreamed of going to. The sun peered over the trees as we approached Pellow Island's beach and I climbed out the chair and stood by David, my eyes fixed on the spectacle before me.

"It's far more beautiful in person," I smiled as I turned to David.

"I don't know; your paintings sure do it justice." His lips turned up into a smirk.

David moored the boat up along the shore and I jumped out onto the hot sand. It was practically empty on the whole island; no one hardly came here; it was one of the reasons why I liked it so much. It was a bubble away from the rest of the world. Despite the high temperature of the place, there was a refreshing breeze and the high trees cast large shadows that hung around us like an icy cave.

"Close your eyes," David said.

I pouted. "I don't want to."

"Close them." He laughed, covering my eyes with his hand as he led me on. I could feel the earth beneath my bare feet change; It was far too hot to wear shoes out here. The sand slowly changed to soil and fallen leaves; I could hear the cracking of twigs as we walked on deep into the forest. Eventually, we stopped. David didn't say anything to me, but I could hear the click of his fingers which followed with a strange amalgamation of sounds, a whistling wind, a crackle of fire, a strong gust of a tornado. David took his hand away from my eyes and I looked before me to see a cosy, wooden cabin. It was high up, with tall stairs that led up to the front door. Its roof nearly reached the top of the trees. I smiled.

"Is this ours?"

David nodded. "All ours."

"For how long?"

He turned to me, his eyes fixed on mine. "For as long as we want."

I grinned instantly running up the stairs. *Wait for me!* I heard him laugh behind me. He took my hand before he led me through the cabin, taking me down the short hallway and into the lounge, which was openly joined to a small kitchen. There was no modern technology of the sort, but in such a beautiful place like this, you didn't need it. The warm oak walls were almost completely filled with bookshelves, packed with novels and short stories and all sorts of biographies. There was one large rectangular window right before us where the

144

sofa stood facing it. It was the perfect cosy spot to relax while reading together. The kitchen was only cut off from the living room by its curved counter, which was topped with a sink and all sorts of teas that I knew David brought for himself. It was a simple set-up, but it was perfect. Back into the hallway, he took me left into the bathroom. It too was small, but it was quaint and cosy. There were two joined sinks before us with a large mirror, the toilet beside it to the right—and opposite that was a huge, deep bath combined with a shower. It was simple and rustic, no modern bathroom blues and whites like it all these houses today. Lastly, he took me into our bedroom, the largest room in the cabin. There was a little study area in the far left, just a small wooden desk with a bookshelf to the side. In the centre of the room was our Wyoming king bed, covered in maroon silk sheets and the same colour cloth draped over the bed from the ceiling to keep it cool at night and to repel the insects. Beyond the bed, the entire back wall was in fact glass. It led out to a small balcony with two comfy chairs for us to sit on and watch the sunset. It had the perfect view of the trees and the ocean in the distance.

David went on to ask me something, but I was not aware of what it was as I dived onto the bed. My body bounced slightly from the spongy mattress, causing a laugh to rumble from my stomach. I looked up to David and his face was at rest. He joined me on the bed, and I snuggled up closer to him, resting my head on his chest.

The sun was just setting when we both awoke around the same time. The sky a watercolour painting of deep reds and oranges that were mixing into an inky purple. We had practically slept the entire day, and still, we felt tempted to the idea of falling back into that comfy darkness. But we remained awake, encouraged by each other's company. My head remained rested upon David's chest as his fingers glided through my hair. I pulled back and leaned up to him, snaking my arms around his neck as I shuffled up closer and pressed my lips to his.

"Mine," I pouted.

David let out a small laugh which was billowing from within him before he turned his chin down to me. "Yours."

"Yours," I returned, the corners of my lips curling up.

He remained still, gazing over my features as though he were admiring an oil painting. Although it flattered me, I also felt embarrassed to be looked at in such a way, as though I was his entire world. Did I deserve to be?

I closed my eyes as I nestled contently against David's chest.

"Here," he said and when I opened my eyes as I was met by my sketchbook. I took it from my hands, staring at it with wide eyes as if he had given me a lost treasure from my childhood. "I brought it along. Would hate for you to stop painting."

I sat up. "Thank you!" I clutched it close to my chest. "But what about my paints?" I spoke with a sheepish smile on his face; I hated to seem ungrateful, but I had to bring up it.

"They're here too." He gestured to the desk in the corner that was now accompanied with various paints, brushes, and pencils upon it.

I looked back to David once I saw all the art equipment.

"I'm sure you're magic."

"Maybe I am." He smiled.

The moon had replaced the sun once we finally ventured outside. Her glow glistened upon the ocean waves to paint her own stars on the earth.

As the tide came in further with each wave, our feet got wetter and wetter as we ran along with it.

We couldn't help but laugh at how childish we were acting, at times I found it uncontrollable, the laughter. The salty water splashed beneath our feet as we continued along the beach that stretched out for miles.

We had no reason to run, we just wanted to.

It was that feeling of complete freedom that brought it on, like when a herd of wild horses begins to gallop around, and why? Because they could. Because they're free to do so.

It was a full moon, and the sky was pitch-black with every star visible in the sky, no sign of clouds. We had been running around for hours.

At one point we ran waist-deep into the sea, laughing and splashing at each other like children.

But as the night grew on, our adrenaline died down.

Our run turned into a walk, which turned into a stroll as our hands linked together. The warm sand dried and stuck to the soles of our feet as we edged further from the waves.

Eventually, our stroll came to a stop and we both dropped down into the soft sand. I practically lay down, with just my elbows keeping me up slightly.

I had no intention of this being a temporary sit down. I lounged over David with my head on his chest, draping my arms around his waist.

"Thank you for bringing me here," I exhaled calmly. "It's always been my dream to come."

"Well, I'm glad I could help make it a dream come true."

I snuggled my head against his chest as my eyes closed. I was beyond exhausted.

"I never want to leave."

"We don't have to," he murmured.

19
Dolor

I awoke only a few hours later.

It was only just starting to get light out.

Beside me, Miles was still fast asleep.

It made me wonder why I wasn't.

But my curiosity was soon answered as a sharp pain ignited in my chest. It caused me to grip the flesh as I groaned.

It was burning.

I felt like I had been stabbed, over and over again, the pain getting worse as time passed.

I quickly got myself out of bed.

I needed air.

The agony was excruciating and made me feel helpless.

Why was I so out of control of my body?

I hadn't felt anything like it before.

I managed to make my way out the cabin, my hand still clutched onto my chest.

As if that helped in any way.

I walked hastily through the thick forest and out onto the beach.

I didn't stop until I reached the tide and at that point, I fell down onto my knees.

Still, the pain was there.

Going around in circles of agony, from excruciating, to mild, back to excruciating.

I looked out upon the waves that appeared to be moving in slow motion; the crashing sound of water upon water seemed to be shallow, echoey.

What is happening to me? I questioned in my head repetitively.

Demons don't feel pain.

Not like this, at least.

I continued to stare out until the pain began to wear out a bit, and it was filled with another sensation—a chill down my spine.

I was not alone.

My attention was instantly captured to my right, and there, he was stood.

Angelus Canticum.

Billy.

He was just stood there, staring at me.

His posture relaxed and mind at peace as he stood there calmly while a strong gust of wind swamped us up from the ocean's force.

"I know who you are," I panted, out of breath from the stress the pain had caused me.

He smiled. "And I you, brother."

I always had a suspicion he did, it explained why he was so protective over Miles. He must've thought me a fool for not knowing who he was the instant I first saw him.

My mockery of myself soon ended as the pain returned in another wave. I winced from its burning and my hand met my chest once again.

"What is happening to me?"

Once again, Billy replied calmly, as though all was right in the world.

"You've given up your kind for love." He seemed pleased. "It won't be long now."

I was changing.

Changing into the very thing I swore never to become.

"No." I protested as I stumbled up onto my feet. "I will not become one of you."

"Too late." Billy smiled.

"David!" Miles called out.

I looked over to where I heard his voice before I turned back to Billy.

But he wasn't there.

He had vanished into thin air.

And with him, my pain had eased once again.

Liar.

I scoffed to myself before I turned to Miles as he came running over.

"What are you doing out here?" He asked.

"I couldn't sleep." I shrugged. "Thought I'd just watch the waves."

"I'll join you."

We stayed sat upon the sand watching the waves until the sun had fully emerged. At that point, Miles became hungry. I had no desire to eat, but I would still happily cook him something.

Miles sat at the kitchen counter as he watched me.

At this point, my pain had faded but I still didn't feel fit to eat.

He questioned my lack of appetite.

I simply said I wasn't hungry and left it at that.

Still, I enjoyed rustling up his breakfast, seeing him smile at the smells he would soon be able to taste.

Before him, I placed a plate of ackee and saltfish, with some premade hard dough bread on the side.

It only seemed right for him to try traditional food of the place we were calling home.

After he had enjoyed his breakfast, he wanted to go out again.

Explore more of the beach, maybe paint.

I was glad.

I felt a lot more comfortable outdoors, which was unusual for me.

The indoors used to be much more to my forte, or at least in Cambridge it was.

But here, staying indoors almost felt claustrophobic when you knew there was so much outside to see.

We showered together before we left.

Miles took a small backpack filled with his sketchbook, pencils, and paints for whenever he found a view he adored, which here didn't take long.

We walked opposite to the beach we were at that morning, heading deeper into the forest to get to the ocean on the other side.

We were in that maze of trees for over an hour, climbing up muddy slopes and jumping across gentle streams.

I was fine for most of it, even though I felt myself getting tired and finding the afternoon heat near unbearable.

I was still fine.

But then the pain kicked back in.

The heat of the day vanished and was replaced by ice in my blood.

The sharp pains thumped along with my heartbeat and pulsed through my veins; it was becoming even more torturous than before.

I struggled to keep up with Miles, but I did my best to keep my composure as he asked if I was all right.

"Yes, yes." I laughed off the pain. "Just the heat."

He agreed it was a struggle before we went on.

Soon, Miles was just a speck in the distance and disappeared behind the trees.

I stumbled on, heading in the same direction Miles had been, following his footsteps in the soil that I could only just make out with my double vision.

I finally made my way out of the forest, bursting through the thick leaves with a gasp for ocean air.

It was a relief to be out.

Soon as I saw Miles sat in the sand, looking out to the crystal-clear sea with his sketchbook and a pencil in hand, the pain seemed to instantly be washed away by the ocean's waves.

"You finally made it." Miles teased.

I laughed and joined him on the sand, crossing my legs and leaning aside to see what he was drawing.

He instantly hid the page from me, holding the sketchbook to his chest.

"It's not finished," he whined.

"Fine, fine." I smiled and turned my attention to the open ocean; I was too tired to bully him into showing me. I let him continue.

We passed several moments in a comfortable silence as he concentrated.

The sound of the crashing waves the only entity filling the empty air.

"Would you stay here?" I asked, finally breaking the silence.

"We *are* staying here." Miles replied, his head down to his sketchbook as he began to paint.

"I mean, forever—with me." I was nervous to ask him, but I needed to do so.

He turned to look at me. "Are you serious?"

I nodded.

It was hard to read his expression for a moment, he was clearly thinking about it—the consequences, the positives, the repercussions, the toll it would have on his future.

Yet he smiled. "If it's with you, I'm happy anywhere."

The volume of my question seemed to have major repercussions that night.

As Miles slept soundly beside me, I couldn't even bear to close my eyes as I lied there in a cold sweat.

I could feel it, the change.

Billy wasn't lying.

Everything inside me was changing, the very fibre of my being slowly swapped out for angel genes.

I didn't want it.

Change frankly scared me.

Why do I have to change to love?

Can't a demon be happy? Be in love?

According to our high powers, apparently not.

But what if it wasn't just my form that changed?

What if being an angel suddenly made me love big crowds and despise my gorgeous camomile tea?

What about the Aston?!

What if becoming an angel made me fall out of love with Miles?

Every possible outcome was waterboarding me and I simply let myself drown in it all.

My body trembled from the cold within.

My constant tossing and turning soon caused Miles to wake.

He was exhausted but that didn't stop him from looking ever so worried as his eyes fell upon me. "What's wrong?"

I didn't know how to explain it.

"I don't feel so good," is all I could manage to say.

He instantly wrapped his arms around me; I could feel him flinch ever so slightly at how cold I was. But still, he pulled me close. "Let's warm you up."

I joined in the exchange and snaked my arms back around him.

With every wince and groan I let out, Miles just embraced me tighter.

Soon, his tactic seemed to work.

I lay there, feeling safe within his arms.

My comfort caused the pain to die down, my body temperature to rise, and my breathing to slow down.

My tight grip around him eased slightly as I relaxed, the heaps of stress and anxiety I felt hit me back in the face with tiredness.

"Sleep," Miles said calmly, pressing a gentle kiss to my forehead before his eyes closed.

I gazed upon him with my sleepy eyes until I couldn't resist.

My vision turned to darkness and soon, my mind was a blank canvas for my dreams.

There was no time for sleepy kisses and loving 'good mornings' the following day.

Something was wrong.

The pain was back, but it wasn't the same—and it wasn't coming from me.

What woke me was the scalding heat.

It was morning but the room was shrouded in darkness.

I shot up to find Nuntius and Perfidus standing at the end of the bed.

They were enraged and it was their mist engulfing the room, their fury making it unbearably hot.

Miles awoke shortly after by my jolting, but to him the room was empty, and the sun was greeting him through the windows.

But the twins were here to end it, they weren't going to let their invisibility to mankind stop them.

Before I told you that they can't talk to humans, they can't be seen nor touched; but they can gain access to the mortal side through those who can.

Those like me.

"Baby, what's wrong?" Miles frowned; he was terrified by my fear.

I couldn't physically answer.

The dark figures' mist twisted in my direction and shot into my chest.

They had full control.

And they could be seen.

I was helpless, I couldn't save Miles from what was to come.

I couldn't comfort him as he screamed and cowered from the demons in his room.

His safe space was gone.

I had taken him to the other side of the world and even here, they tracked us down.

The twins forced me out of bed, my body moving without me as I remained caged in my mind.

They had me stand between them as the smoke of their souls overwhelmed me.

Now they were kicking down the doors in my mind, and it didn't take long for them to get inside.

I could feel their darkness snaking through all my thoughts, all my secrets, all of my memories.

I was in their full control, nothing but a puppet.

They spoke through me, exposing my true self to Miles; why I was here, why I was with him.

"You were simply a task I let go on for too long," is what they made me say. "You are only one of many I've had to deal with."

Miles didn't seem to believe any of it at first, he probably thought it was all a bad dream.

But they forced me to go into detail, bringing in how I became his professor—the countless people I killed, the lies I told. But of course, they kept out the current truth, that I gave up my old ways because I truly loved him. That, they tossed aside, focussing and making me say only the wrongs I had committed.

Even with them having complete power over me, I could feel Miles' pain. I could sense his distress and the sorrow on his face showed that their evil game was working: his heart was breaking.

Miles' heart had cracked open, exposed.

The twins could smell it.

They tossed me aside and latched onto the love of my afterlife, sucking out all of the happiness from his soul. Draining him of all that was good within him and leaving him an empty shell.

"Miles," I could feel my own blackened heart break as I looked upon his limp body, his eyes heavy and red from crying.

They had taken my sweet Miles away from me.

And once again, there was nothing I could do.

The mission was done.

The wooden floor creaked and rumbled beneath my feet.

"No!" I yelled as the ground heated up and slid open beneath me.

"Miles!" I leapt forward in hope to change my fate, but it had already been chosen for me.

The twins clung onto my ankles and tugged me down, pulling me back down into the depths of Hell.

I had fallen.

20
Dolor

I bet you imagined Hell being some sort of dark, reeking cave burning in scorching red fire.

Well, you were wrong.

The depictions you see in these 'moving photographs' have got it all backwards.

As much as I hate to say it, Satan has taste.

A cave it may be.

And yes, it was ridiculously hot down there, especially to newbies.

But there was no bloodshot lava, no dreadful stench.

Hell was set out like a maze.

To those who had no purpose down there, this was made to make them endlessly lose themselves within it until they went mad.

For demons, however, they could easily find their way around and all had their own private quarters.

We were treated like royalty, really.

The walls were of thick marble that contained the pulsing violet lava that brought the place to a dim glow. It fed through all the walls like veins.

Yes, it was really quite beautiful.

But apart from Hell's modern aesthetic, it was simply dull.

The only sounds were of the screams of those who had gone mad, and of the low rumbling of the lava travelling through the marble.

It was the loneliest place to be, and yet you always felt you were being watched.

I hated being back.

And by no surprise, I wasn't greeted with praise and allowed to return to my tranquil quarters of Victorian splendour.

I was imprisoned.

Tossed aside, I was trapped within a small cube room with absolutely nothing in it apart from a slab of more marble in the right-hand corner which was supposedly a bed.

Not even a pillow.

Gits.

Frankly, I didn't want any better.

I didn't deserve to be treated well and drowned in luxury.

Not because I went against orders, but because I'd hurt Miles.

Not on purpose, but I'd still lied to him. I'd still kept my true self a secret, and this was the consequence.

I deserved the loneliness, the pain. The sorrow.

What should have I done differently?

Everything, really.

I should've told Miles what we were running away from.

I should've told him who I really was as soon as I fell for him; I let things go too far.

I should've stopped myself from falling for him in the first place because the result always ends in pain.

But hooray to me, the Demon of Heartache and Pain, I had succeeded.

Step 6 of being an absolute arsehole: Break their heart.

Check.

I was sick of it, sick of myself.

If only I was alive, I thought.

If only I grew up around the same time as Miles, I would've treated him right—like a prince.

If only, if only, if only…

But none of it mattered.

I could wish all I wanted; I could plead that I was a good man, that I was the right one for Miles.

If only I had a second chance, I would make things right.

Enough!

I gripped my fingers in my hair, tugging at it roughly in frustration as I sat upon that excuse of a bed.

I could wish, I could beg, I could even pray all I wanted.

My words would not help me down below.

Forgiveness—everyone deserves it, they say.

But really?

Even a demon?

Yeah, didn't think so.

Enough was enough.

I nodded to myself in agreement that I couldn't look back.

I loved Miles but I wasn't getting him back now.

I had to move on.

In this place you only have two options: go mad, or cause madness.

I had to close my heart back up and toss away the key.

My only way back into my co-workers' good books was by showing I could be that same demon I was those many moons ago.

That I could once again be that fearsome fiend they all knew me as.

I only hoped Miles would understand, and that one day he'd find a better man than I am.

God knows he deserved it.

I removed my fingers from my dark locks and wiped off the wetness from my face. I would not cry over this boy.

I sat up straight, leaning against the wall lightly as I closed my eyes.

I would not submit to my emotions.

I would not be weakened by love.

I would not expose my heart to anyone, especially a human.

Especially him.

It had only been five hours.

Five hours of me sitting contently upon that stone bed when my restful mind had been disturbed, corrupted.

Something within me was fighting against my best efforts to forget Miles.

It was the pain.

The same pain from back on the beach.

How it still managed to continuously stab me in the heart, I do not know even to this day.

But there it was.

Mild at first, I managed to keep it at bay with the clenching of my teeth turning my hands into fists.

But soon it became unbearable, my quiet winces quickly turned to painful groans. The cold sweat returned; my body was so cold that I began to burn up.

The pain had never been this bad before.

I was panicked by it, my breathing rapid. With my knees up to my chest, I hugged my legs tightly in the hope that the pain would soon stop.

But it only got worse.

You've given up your kind for love.

Billy's words spun around my head, mixed within the agony.

He was right.

And no matter how much I tried to block it out, I was still deeply in love with Miles, I simply couldn't help it.

He was changing me, and it was only at that moment that I realised; it was for the better.

I let go.

Let go of the hate, of the regret, the pain, the sorrow I had been holding onto for all of my existence.

And with that, the pain washed over me in solid waves that illuminated my body.

I was astonished by the sight of my hands glowing a warm orange.

But soon the light was too strong, and my eyes were forced closed as my whole form shone until I was nothing but a white silhouette, completely engulfed by my own light.

It burned, but only for a few moments and then the light covering me was gone just as quickly as it appeared.

My transformation to the other side was invisible.

I looked myself down, patting my hands over my torso to find no physical difference.

Still, I wore my favourite dark formal attire.

I was still a slender, tall gentleman with my hair just the way I left it.

But I could feel it: it was on the inside. I had changed.

I felt free.

My emotions happily burst through the damns they cowered behind for so long.

I had felt this before, but not in such a high dose.

To feel everything without fear, without worry.

Had all demons just been afraid to reveal their true selves?

Had they stayed in the dark because they were afraid of what the light would show them?

I felt weightless within my light; love.

I just needed to give it back to the one I know needed it most.

I stood and rushed my way over to the thick marble door and hit my fists against it but there was no hope. The touch of the door, in fact, singed my knuckles, I didn't belong down there any more, every touch to my bare skin of Hell's surface was like poison.

Even when I myself had become the light, I still seemed to be stuck in the dark.

I was ashamed to give up so quickly as I sat back down on that ghastly bed.

I had only just become an angel and already I was a pathetic excuse of one.

Some soldier of God I was! I would most likely become a demon again in a few minutes.

There I sat pitying myself, wasting away precious time I could've spent trying to get out, trying to get to Miles and saving him from the darkness corrupting his heart.

But no. I sat, with my head down, eyes staring at the floor.

My time of feeling sorry for myself though was interrupted by my curiosity.

There was a sound, a new sound.

It was no rumble of the living walls.

No scream from a madman.

A howl.

Faint at first but it gradually grew.

I stood just as the sudden sound of guitars and drums bleared through the hallways.

I had a hunch, but it was impossible.

But there it was, my hope raised within me as I heard the sound of tires screeching against the floor, the music getting louder, closer as the resonance of that familiar engine came into hearing range.

I stood against the back wall just in time as bursting through the marble was my beloved Aston.

She hadn't given up on me.

"You beauty!" I exclaimed, quickly brushing off the debris from her bonnet before I got myself back behind the steering wheel where I missed being ever so much, it was like going back home.

With electric guitars still thriving through the speakers, many demons had been alerted by the Aston's rescue mission and were after us.

She had other plans, however.

I had my hands gripping the steering wheel, but she was still in full control as she drove straight through countless more walls, hitting into and throwing aside many demons who tried to stop her.

It was quite humiliating on my part, while she was busy being a hero, I was concerned with the damage done to her paint job by all this demolition.

Nevertheless, no scratch or dent bothered the Aston and soon we were racing our way out of that dark place.

Miles, we are coming for you.

The Aston had given me back control once we were back on the earth's surface, but still, I did not slow down.

Countless times I was on the wrong side of the road, trying to overtake old ladies in their Volvos.

Speed the bloody hell up!

It was nice to know my level of impatience and frustration was still the same, I suppose.

I had only been to Miles' dorm once, but luckily, I remembered where the student building was.

I brought the Aston to a halt outside upon the curb.

I was rushing frantically.

Flat 27.

I remembered that.

"It's out of service!" a passing student called as I bolted my way into the elevator. I didn't care if I was showing my powers, or what any stranger thought. I had to get to Miles quickly.

I was about to click my fingers, but already the elevator doors closed, and I was heading up to the second-highest floor in the building.

Strange.

Powers for angels must've worked differently.

All I had to do was think.

The doors opened once I reached the floor, and I wasted no time getting myself to his door.

I knocked, and knocked, and knocked once more until the door opened and my hand was left briefly hitting against thin air.

My face dropped when it wasn't Miles standing there. It was Billy.

"Where is he?" I tried my best to stay calm, but my throat tightened, my words strained.

Billy looked at me sternly.

"In his room." He was being blunt too, rude even. "What are you doing here? I thought you went home."

I shook my head, "That's not my home any more."

I tried pushing passed Billy to get inside, but his wide frame easily stopped me from doing so.

"I need to see him!"

"Why? So you can hurt him even more?" He pushed me back into the hallway. "He's dying in there and there's nothing I can do! It's your fault."

"Please, let me fix this," I begged. "I didn't mean to hurt him; you must know that's the truth. If I was planning on hurting him, why was I changing?" Billy's eyes remained on me, but he wasn't looking, he wasn't focussed. His gaze darted slightly as he thought.

"Why have I changed? Even after what happened…"

Still, he did not respond, and a threatening silence grew between us that frightened me, I had to dispel it.

"I love him," was all I could manage.

Billy was becoming agitated, battling between the truth he was told of and the one before his eyes.

I was lucky, he knew me. He knew better.

"You fix this," he said defeatedly, moving aside to let me through.

I wasted no time in getting past.

The sight of Miles was heart-wrenching as I entered his room.

His skin was as pale as a sheet.

His expression emotionless, one of tiredness and distress.

What had I done?

I kneeled by the side of his bed as I took his flaccid hand in mine, gripping it in hopes of a response, but there was nothing. He remained lifeless.

"I'm sorry." The pointless words spilt out of me, in light of the fact that I knew they meant nothing, they were the only words I could conjure up. "I'm so, so sorry, Miles."

Still, there was no response as I placed myself on the edge of Miles' bed and hauled him onto my lap, only his eyes flustering open ever so slightly by the fact he was being moved around.

I felt helpless as I pleaded my apologises to him.

I needed my Miles back, but I was more than unsure of how to do so.

I turned to Billy who was leaning against the doorframe, his arms folded as he looked upon us. He almost looked disappointed in me for not knowing what to do.

But I didn't.

I had never been an angel before,

I had never saved someone from the darkness of their hearts before.

"Save him," he said simply as if that would help me somehow.

I shook my head in my state of helplessness.

"I don't know how. I've never done this before."

"You don't need to be an angel to save him, Dolor."

I was puzzled still, but a part of me knew it made complete sense.

He continued. "Give him back what was taken from him."

Of course.

How could I have been so stupid?

The demons had ripped love out of Miles.

Love, trust, faith—all of the things that I had caused to build up in him over the past few months, suddenly stripped away.

My eyes fell upon Miles.

His sweet, soft face that had been masked with darkness.

A darkness only I could remove.

I was slow, delicate, in leaning down to connect our lips while my hands cupped his face.

I didn't know what would come of this, or if it would even work.

But I believed Billy that I could save him.

I had to.

And I did.

Before I knew it, my body was engulfed by a gentle orange glow once more.

Only this time, it affected Miles too.

His skin radiated with the same glow I was emitting and soon it was too bright to keep my eyes open.

It got brighter and brighter and I held Miles tighter and tighter.

This was it.

The return of Miles' love.

The true Miles to look me in the eyes and see me for what I really was: his.

I glow lessened as I felt his lips push back against mine.

He was back.

Miles slowly pulled away as he looked up at me, he still looked terribly weakened by it all, but the colour in his cheeks returned and his eyes had that small glimmer in them I always adored.

"You lied to me." His voice cracked as he spoke; he was furious. But his anger came out in tears rather than aggression.

"No," I started, not even knowing why I said that. It soon became clear to me though. "I was lying to myself."

And I was.

For so long I convinced myself that shutting myself off from the world would make me stronger.

Yet I had never felt more alive than when I was with him.

"I may have followed the darkness my whole life, but you made me see the goodness in the light. You may have started as just some mission, but I did fall in love with you and I ran away from the truth, hid it away so I could be with you."

He stared at me.

Silence.

"I don't expect forgiveness—"

"I do forgive you," Miles interrupted. "As much as I try to hate you, I can't help but love you. But please, this time I want to know the real you."

I smiled. "You always have. In fact, I believe you know me more than I know myself."

Miles shut me up with a kiss.

I felt safe to know despite everything, he still wanted me to keep his heart.

Billy pulled me aside into the apartment's tiny kitchen once Miles and I parted from our kiss.

I felt like I was in trouble, being sent to the headmaster's office.

"He doesn't need me any more," he said plainly, but there was a smile on his face; he looked free.

"What are you talking about?"

"Miles," he clarified. "He doesn't need me any more. You're his guardian angel now, more than that, in fact." The smile remained on his lips as his hand found my shoulder. "And I do believe he's in safe hands."

"He still needs you. You're his friend."

Billy nodded, "That I am. But that doesn't change the fact; it's time for me to go."

There were times when I rebelled against the very thing Billy was doing at that moment, I fought to stay on earth.

But the fact of the matter is that angels and demons can't stay.

Once they've completed what they set out to do, they must return home whether they like it or not.

They either walk there or get dragged there.

"You can't stay forever," Billy reminded me in a stern voice.

"I know." I nodded. "I'll be back soon. I just need time with him."

He nodded; he understood the importance of time spent with a loved one, especially when that time is so clearly numbered.

Yet he didn't say goodbye, to me or Miles.

Not because he didn't want to, he simply ran out of time.

I returned to Miles. Of course, he asked where Billy went.

"Home," I said. "He went home."

21
Miles

I stayed with David back in the manor over the summer months. I had no intention going back to see my family, especially now knowing my time with David was limited.

Every night was comforting to fall asleep in his arms.

Every morning was blissful to see him lying there beside me. I would watch him as he slept, the sun always cast his face so beautifully during those early hours.

I was devastated when he first told me our time together was numbered. Since then I always appreciated the simple things with him. Even things like this, a lie-in in the morning. I would take mental pictures in my mind to hold on to forever. That, and my sketchbook, which was now full of paintings I drew of our special times together.

It was a rainy Thursday evening when David took me to a small café down the road from the university. I reserved us the table by the window. I loved how the rain ran down against it, the way the lights in the distance would reflect off them.

"Am I interrupting something?" David laughed as he approached, placing down our drinks and food.

"Only my imagination." I smirked. I took my coffee from the tray and had a sip before David slid his drink towards me.

"Want a taste?"

It was his usual order of camomile tea. I nodded before I held the cup with both my hands and took a sip. David laughed as he saw my surprised delight. It was delicious.

"How have I never tried this before?"

We stayed there till closing time when the waitress had pulled up all the over chairs over the tables.

We gave her a reasonable tip for letting us stay so late, even when we had finished our tea and slices of cake so long ago.

It was pitch-black out by the time we left, but luckily the rain had stopped. David drove us on to the same forest where we first got to know each other. And just like the first time, we lied down watching the world go by as we listened to music from the car stereo.

"The last time we were here I was a very different man," David said.

I turned to him. "You mean because you were a demon?"

"In a way. It was here I began to question who I was. What I stood for." He paused, turning to me, "It was here I no longer saw you as just a mission. I saw you as the bright, adorable man you are."

I laughed, "Adorable?"

He simply laughed too and wrapped his arms around me, bringing me into his lap.

We only had a few days left now and it was sinking in, for both of us.

I could tell by the forced smile on David's face that following morning that he was hurting, that he was dreading to be without me.

I couldn't let us end on such a sad note.

"I want to take you somewhere today." I tried to distract him from his thoughts. I wanted to go to the bookstore, to show him where I spent a lot of my time, even more so now that it was my place of work over the summer. It was only part-time, but it was the money I needed to start my new life.

After our time was up, I wouldn't bring myself to stay here. I applied to take my Master's degree in New York and I got in. Now it was just getting there.

I only wished David could go with me, comfort me as I travelled to a new, strange place.

We walked to the bookstore; it wasn't too far from the manor.

I worked Monday to Wednesday. I would always make sure David woke up to a sweet note I left early in the morning.

When I came home in the evening, David always had dinner ready for me on the table and we would talk for hours about each other's day.

It was a small independent store in a rustic stone building, three floors high; new books, non-fiction, autobiographies and travel on the ground floor, fiction filled the second floor and the owner of the store lived on the top floor.

"About time we met." The shop owner grinned excitedly as she shook David's hand. "Mai."

"David," he returned.

"Oh, I know who you are. Miles doesn't shut up about you," she laughed, bringing me to an embarrassed smile.

"Well, enjoy looking around, I trust Miles will look after you."

"He always does." David smiled at her as she left.

I took David's hand and led him upstairs to where all the fiction was kept, and there we spend hours rooting through the shelves, conferring with each other on books we liked, books we didn't, discussing what we thought, what we believed.

"What are you still doing here?" Mai gasped on her way up to her apartment. "It's eight-thirty!"

We had lost track of time massively as we got caught up in the world of books.

We apologised and tided up the books we left lying around before we left Mia in peace.

22
Dolor

Last day left.

It had all gone so quickly.

Miles' things were all packed ready for America and soon I would be on my way to my new home.

I woke up early and took Miles' sketchbook from the side. He refused to pack it, he wanted to carry it, keep it close at all times.

I understood why, soon I would be gone, and this sketchbook would be the only piece he had of me.

There was only one page left blank, and there I left him a note I hoped he would treasure for the rest of his days until he returned to me in the sky. I was quick to get it done without him seeing, even though there ended up being no point in doing so as he awoke an hour or so after.

That day was quiet.

Filled with the inevitable loss we would both soon feel.

We had a small breakfast then returned to bed where we lounged for hours lost within each other's arms.

How I'd miss the smoothness of his skin, the softness of his silky curls, his smile that lit up every room.

We said very little to each other, afraid of bringing up the very thing we were dreading.

But I didn't mind, his touch was all I needed.

His touch, the rare joy you feel when a butterfly lands on your hand. Something you knew couldn't last forever even though while it was happening in the moment, it felt like centuries were passing by.

This, his touch, his hands, his lips, his eyes, the very essence of his being; I wish I could bottle it up in a jar and take with me, as I wish I could bottle up a piece of me and give it to him.

But our day would come again, I did not doubt that.

It was later that evening as we lay together upon the sofa that I knew it was time.

My name was beginning to be called by a new voice.

My new home.

I looked down at Miles as he rested upon my chest. "It's time."

"No." He looked up at me. "A little longer."

I shook my head.

"Oh, my love." A sad smile crept onto my face, one that led to the build-up of tears. "I can't."

He hugged me, one so tight. The very kind you give when you know it'll be the last.

But it wouldn't be, and I needed him to know that.

"You'll be seeing me again, my love." I placed his sketchbook upon his lap. "You keep this close, and you bring it back to me when we next meet."

I tilted up his chin, so he was looking at me, the tears running down his cheeks I wiped away with my thumbs.

"Wherever you go, whatever happens—I will be watching over you. I will always be in here." I rested my hand gently over his heart.

"Breathing as one?" He tried to smile, in the hope of my response.

I echoed his words, "Breathing as one."

I left not long after, my lips were still pressed against Miles as the glow around me embraced me, it took me home. I wasted no time in looking around or meeting my new co-workers. I found Billy.

"Here," he said once I found him, he already set up a way for me to watch over Miles.

I kneeled as I peered at the still pool, a window to earth, to Miles.

He was crying, but I could see a smile on his face as I leaned my hand down into the water, tracing over his cheek. He immediately touched it, feeling the breeze of my presence.

He knew I was still there.

In his hands he clutched onto the sketchbook, which was opened, he was already looking through it, reminiscing on our times together.

He reached the last page.

And now Miles, I watch over you.
Your guardian angel, your love.
All I ask is you do not live your life in my shadow.
Live to the fullest, my clever boy.
I'll always be here for you, waiting.
And when you feel alone, when you question if I am still there, you look to the stars at night, and you'll see me staring right back.
We will forever breathe as one,
Our inferno hearts will forever beat in unison.